The Lady Flyer

by

Jane Lewis

The Lady Flyer

Cover Art by *The Wild Rose Press, Inc.*

The Wild Rose Press, Inc.
PO Box 708
Adams Basin, NY 14410-0708
Visit us at www.thewildrosepress.com

Publishing History
First Vintage Rose Edition, 2020
Print ISBN 978-1-5092-2943-7
Digital ISBN 978-1-5092-2944-4

Published in the United States of America

He stared at the lake he flew over each time he landed at the airfield, stopped the car, and turned off the ignition. "Your uncle's lake?"

"Yes, there's a bench where we can sit and talk."

He opened her door and put his arm around her waist drawing her close. Twilight gave enough light for him to see the bench close to the water. He waited for her to sit and then he sat, held her hand and placed a kiss on her cheek. He stared at the sky as the stars came out one by one. "This is a magical place."

She placed her hand on the back of his neck and pulled his face close.

He gazed into her eyes. The jolt of his gut reaction unnerved him. She'd been sealed in his heart since the day he met her and if he kissed her the way his lips wanted there would be no going back. Her mouth enticed him, soft and willing. Instead of kissing her lips, he placed a chaste kiss on the top of her head. She put her arms around his neck, her body melted into his. Every woman before her, every disappointment, every happiness sabotaged by her embrace. He brushed kisses on the velvet skin of her neck and obeyed his heart. He fell into her snare and captured her mouth, devouring the sweetness of her lips, her response as eager as his.

Jane Lewis' Previous Releases

LOVE AT FIVE THOUSAND FEET
and
THE BARNSTORMER

Dedication

To my sweet husband, Billy, my real-life hero

An aviator "must be of the male gender."
~*Louis Bauer, Aviation Medicine-1926*
Office of U. S. Surgeon General

Chapter One

Saplingville, Georgia
June 1939

The roar of the approaching airplane cut through the morning fog. Lisbeth Douglas climbed off the step ladder, walked to the front of the hangar and joined her brother. She wiped the grease from her hands on her overalls. "I'm done with the Staggerwing."

"Good, check out the Cessna. Frankie said he heard a knock in the engine." Victor gazed at the sky. "I hope he lands, maybe he'll need fuel. I could use some extra money for the payroll this week."

"Sounds like a hell of a big plane." She twirled around, searching in all directions through the breaks in the haze. "I see it."

The airplane floated through the ground clouds. Victor pointed toward the sky. "It's a Beechcraft Model 18 Twin Beech, the same size as the Tri-Motor. More than likely on their way to Atlanta."

The large aircraft made a smooth landing, taxied down the runway, and stopped by the tie down next to the Stinson Tri-Motor.

She studied the plane from the twin engines and low wings to the tailwheel. "Man, I'd love to fly that ship."

"Me and you both. Let's check it out."

She walked with her brother toward the airplane.

A young man climbed from the cockpit dressed like a dandy. His handsome face accented by his dapper suit and tie stopped her in her tracks.

Lisbeth examined her coveralls and stared at her hands and nails black with grease from the airplane engine. "You go on. I need to go back inside."

She hurried to the bathroom wishing she had a change of clothes. She scrubbed her hands clean but the stains on her uniform proved impossible to remove. *I look like a rag-a-muffin.* "Damn." Since she started working for her brother, she dressed like one of the boys in her coveralls and hat. She only dressed up on the weekends for church or a date. She stuffed the memory of her last date in the file drawer of her mind labeled 'Do Not Open.' She sniffed at the sleeve, she smelled of motor oil, grease and sweat.

Lisbeth came out of the bathroom and ran toward the Cessna. She had enough time to climb the ladder and stick her head in the engine before they came into the hangar.

"I want you to meet my sister," Victor informed the man. "She's a pilot and mechanic."

The man laughed. "A female pilot and mechanic, hooey. I hope you check her work when she's done."

"I'm quite proud of my little sister. She knows what she's doing, in the air and on the ground." He stopped in front of the airplane. "If anything, she should check our work."

Heat flooded her face, scorching words rose to her throat; she stepped off the ladder and confronted the man. She stuck her hand out, hoping to get some grease on the jerk. "Hi, I'm Lisbeth Douglas, and you are?"

Paul stared at the girl's greasy fingers. "If you don't mind, I'd rather not get my suit dirty. I have an appointment later today in Savannah. But it's nice to meet you. I'm Paul Williams."

Lisbeth lowered her arm and presented him with a scathing glare before she turned and headed up the step ladder. She wiped the sweat off her face with the back of a hand. "Did you have anything else to say to me, Mr. Williams?"

"No, ma'am, not now." He turned toward Victor. "I'd like to talk to you about something."

"We can discuss it in my office." Victor glanced at his sister.

Paul examined the space. "How many people work here?"

Victor responded. "There are four of us. I own the business. Frankie Howard and Lisbeth service planes, teach lessons and fly air taxis. Al Gregory's the handy man, although sometimes I think he runs the place. You gonna need fuel today?"

Paul pulled his money clip from his pocket. "Yes, I do."

Victor directed orders to his sister. "Lisbeth, get Al. He's helping Frankie service the Jenny. Tell him to fuel Mr. Williams' plane."

She nodded at her brother and climbed off the ladder, placing her tools on the table. "Arrogant piece of shit." She mumbled not caring if she was overheard.

She headed toward the pasture, where the JN-Four bi-plane rested in the shed. The men ambled toward her. Frankie pulled the wagon loaded with tools.

She ran through the field. The last time she flew the Jenny, she almost stepped on a black snake, so she ran fast and stepped high. "Al, some man needs fuel for his airplane."

"We decided to head back and work on the Jenny this afternoon." Frankie walked faster. "I wanted to see the airplane. We watched him fly over and land. What kind is it?"

"It's a Twin Beech." She stayed with Al and let her brother-in-law move ahead.

"Man, I've seen pictures of those. Wish I could fly it." The wagon hit a hole. Frankie stopped to pick up a screwdriver.

Al grabbed the handle. "You go on, Missy, and I'll bring the tools." Al raised an eyebrow and studied her. "What's eating you?"

"Nothing."

"Someone's put a bee in your bonnet." Al stopped and gave her his all-knowing grin.

She continued walking, then turned to face him. "I'm. Fine."

"Says you." Al chuckled and guided the wagon over the tall grass. A garden snake slid by.

"Son of a…" She ran toward the airfield. She hated snakes. She always double checked any open cockpit airplane she flew, in case. Mice frolicked in the hay field and snakes loved mice. Black snakes were the norm, but every once in a while, she came across a copperhead soaking up the heat from the sun. She ran in the hangar and climbed the step ladder.

She continued her work on the Cessna and glanced into the office. The man opened his briefcase and removed papers. Victor read the pages before he picked up a pen and signed. Al and Frankie walked in the office. Her brother made introductions and the men shook hands.

Her co-workers left the boss' office; she followed them outside. "Do either of you know why this guy came to Saplingville?"

The old man smiled; his eyes flashed knowledge. "Says his name is Paul Williams. He's a handsome dude, don't you think so?"

She kept her features deceptively composed. "Typical man, doesn't think a woman can do anything."

The men glanced at each other. Frankie said, "Well, he doesn't know our Lisbeth now, does he?"

"Don't try to calm me down. You should have heard what he said about me." She crossed her arms ready to argue.

"I gotta fuel the airplane before the boss fires me." Al walked toward the airplane with Frankie.

Lisbeth spoke loudly to get her brother-in-law's attention. "Let Al do that himself. I need help getting the Staggerwing out, so I can do a test flight."

Frankie said something to Al and poked him in the ribs. He walked toward her, his mouth twisting into a half smile. "Let's get the airplane out of the hangar."

She climbed in the bi-plane and ran through her pre-flight checklist, taxied down the runway, and lifted off. The radial engine purred from her expert tuning. She retracted the landing gear, sailed through the air and watched the speed until it cruised at one hundred seventy-five miles per hour. Hell, she'd been with Frankie when he cruised at two hundred miles per hour. She swallowed saliva to quench her dry throat and tightened her grip on the wheel. The Staggerwing blew through the clouds reaching a cruising speed of two hundred one miles per hour. Her shouts of laughter filled the plane. "I'm doing it; I can fly faster than Frankie." She relaxed in her seat and let the bi-plane soar. Guilt of using precious fuel made her head back to the airfield. On her descent, a taxicab pulled into the parking lot. Paul Williams climbed in the back seat and the car headed toward town.

She landed and taxied toward the large hangar where they kept their fleet of planes. The men helped her settle the Beech Staggerwing in the hangar. Al placed the chocks under each wheel.

"How'd she fly?" Frankie ran his hand over the wing.

"I got to a cruising speed of two hundred one." She grinned at her brother-in-law.

"No shit?" He grabbed the tie-down rope.

"Yeah, now I fly faster than you." She picked up the clipboard. "Did you find out why that man was here?"

"No, but the boss wants to see all of us in his office." Frankie tied a knot in the rope to secure the plane. "This speed contest isn't over either," Frankie said as he hurried toward the hangar.

Lisbeth walked with Al, anxious to find out who the man was and what he wanted in Saplingville.

Victor stood and smiled at his crew. "Come in, pull up a chair."

She put her hands on her hips. "Who the hell is he?"

His voice rang with command. "Have a seat and I'll tell ya." He sat in his chair and motioned for everyone to sit.

She stood her ground. "I heard him insult my abilities. I don't screw up; people could die."

"Take a seat, Lisbeth."

A warning voice whispered in her head. She followed his orders and sat. Her brother, a former bomber pilot, ran his business with military precision. He trained her and depended on her expertise.

He waited for the crew to settle in their seats. "He's an airplane salesman for Beech Aircraft. He wants to use Saplingville as his home base for the Southeast. I called Ella and got him a room at the boarding house. He plans to travel most of the time."

"And when he isn't traveling?" She met his determined gaze without flinching.

A shadow of annoyance crossed his face. "He's renting a space in this hangar. All he needs is a little desk in the corner with a telephone."

He nodded toward Al. "I need you to get him set up."

Al put his cap on and stood. "Sure, I'll get right on it."

Victor stood. "Guys, I need to speak with my sister privately. Close the door on your way out." Her brother sat and glared at her.

She raised her chin, a defiant sneer settled on her face. "You're going to let him work here?" She knew she should shut up, but anger simmered, and the words poured out. "You accept him, just like that, into our lives, our work."

"It's business. If we don't welcome him, he'll find another airport. This is a Godsend; our resources are low right now and if things don't pick up, I'll have to let you go. Frankie and I have a wife and kids depending on us. You live at home and I don't think you understand the pressures we face supporting a family and running a business." He folded his arms across his chest.

Panic pierced her gut. What would she do without flying? Work as a clerk in a store? Hell, no. "I'm sorry." Her apology sincere.

Her brother nodded his understanding. "I told you when you started this career it wouldn't be easy. You're a woman in a man's world. Some men feel threatened by you. Even if you are my sister, you're beautiful and smart. It's hard for men to see past that. What was the theme of the Female Flight Conference in Atlanta?"

She stared at the floor remembering when she met Amelia Earhart. "Persevere and believe in yourself." She met her brother's gaze; his sincerity caused her lip to quiver. "It's harder than I thought."

"Amelia Earhart must have dealt with a bunch of pig-headed men. You can, too. I know how her disappearance a month after you met her has influenced all your choices. You've accomplished more in the last two years than most people in their lifetime."

She removed her hat and placed it in her lap. Her hair fell toward her face as she fixed her gaze on the floor. "I hoped convincing Pa and Ma to let me fly instead of attending college would be the only obstacle. Boy, was I wrong."

Victor shuffled through his top drawer. "Are we good?" He pulled out a map and notepad.

The meeting was over, and she'd lost. She swallowed the defeat, her voice drifted to a whisper. "We're good."

Chapter Two

Paul climbed in the back seat of the nineteen twenty-six black and yellow Studebaker taxicab.

The driver put the car in first gear and headed to the country road. "Where to?"

"Take me to Ella's Boarding House, please." He twisted in his seat, so he could see the Red Staggerwing touch down. He knew Lisbeth sat at the controls, her landing smooth as glass.

"Ella's Boarding House, right away, sir. Mind if I leave the windows down? We're in for a scorcher today."

He loosened his tie. "The windows down are fine. The air feels good. I'm Paul Williams, what's your name?"

"Charles Montgomery. Pleased to meet you. Where ya from?"

"Wichita, Kansas. I work for Beech Aircraft Company. My home base is Saplingville, but I'll travel during the week."

The taxi pulled onto the road; an older gentleman stood in his front yard beside a truck. The man waved, and the taxi driver yelled, "Hi, Walter."

Paul waved at the man. "Who is that gentleman? His house sits close to the airport."

Charles shifted into high gear, the car sailed down the country road. "The airport's on his land. Victor's his nephew. He gave him the land for the airport. He still has enough to farm. He owns the pastures across the road with the cows grazing."

He admired the scenery. Some cows rested under the large oak trees and others fed on grass. A large bull stood near the fence as if guarding his harem. "Nice farm. How much farther to town?"

"Twenty minutes."

He settled in his seat. The hot air circulated through the windows and sweat beaded on his forehead. The lush grass, huge pine trees, horses and too many cows to count flooded his senses. The farmland appeared immaculately cared for and the animals went about the business of eating and resting.

The image of the feisty girl with the biggest blue eyes, he'd ever seen engulfed his thoughts. She was tiny; he couldn't imagine her flying a plane, but she commanded the air in the Beech Staggerwing and landed smoother than he could. He let his imagination drift to what she would look like out of her greasy coveralls. Was her hair long or short? Was her body luscious and curvy under her coveralls or stick thin?

As they neared the city, the houses stood close together and people meandered down sidewalks. "Charles, before you take me to the boarding house, drive through the city."

The driver peered in his rearview mirror. "Ain't much of a town, just a Main Street."

"Take me down Main Street. I want to see where I'll live for the next few months."

The cabbie turned down the main thoroughfare. "That, there is the drugstore. Victor's father, Jacob, started it many years ago. It's now owned by Jacob

Douglas and Ned Ayers. We've got a five-and-dime, a men's store, a ladies boutique and jewelry store. There's a grocery and a few restaurants, nothing fancy. We're not a fancy town."

A storefront theater with the sign Ruth Ann Howard, Theater and Dance Studio caught his eye. "Is that a movie theater?"

"No, the movie house is two streets over. Victor's sister Ruth Ann owns this place. She went to Atlanta and learned how to become an actress, came back here and opened her drama house. Did you meet Frankie?"

"Yes, he works at the airfield."

"Well, Ruth Ann's his wife."

He surveyed the businesses on Main Street. "Boy, this is a small town."

"This is it; I'll turn around and head to the boarding house. Want me to wait and take you any place else?"

"Yes, wait for me while I meet Ella and get my room. Victor said Ella was his wife's stepmother?"

"Yep, she married Dottie's father."

"I hope I can keep everyone straight. You have to be careful what you say around here."

Charles shifted into low gear, turned on a side street and parked in front of a two-story house. "Oh, yeah, no secrets in this town, everyone knows everybody."

He exited the taxicab and walked up the front walk. A strong perfume smell overwhelmed him. He turned and stuck his head in the car window. "What's the sweet smell?"

Charles pointed to a shrub. "The smell's coming from a gardenia bush. We have lots of them in town."

He investigated the surroundings. Two gardenia bushes stood near the porch where bees competed for the nectar. Zinnias grew beside the walk; a blue butterfly perched fanning its wings. His mother's flower garden had lots of zinnias. The boarding house was a white clapboard house with a large front porch. The floor of the porch was painted red. A swing, bench and a few chairs occupied the area of the porch shaded by a large oak tree. Sunshine filled the other side and supplied the necessary light for several large pots spilling with flowers and green plants. He climbed the steps and knocked on the screen door.

Ella greeted him with a smile as she eased the door open. "Come in, you must be Paul."

"Yes, Paul Williams, nice to meet you."

"Pleasure to meet you. Victor said you need a room?"

"Yes, I'll spend weekends here and I need somewhere to keep my things. Don't know how long I'll live in Saplingville, though."

"No problem, we can accommodate you. I have a corner room upstairs. There are two windows, so the bedroom is cooler at night. Would you like to see it?"

"Yes, please."

He followed Ella up the stairs. "Nice house you have here."

"This is home and I'm happy to share with nice folks. The bathroom is on the left and your room is straight ahead."

He entered a room with a bed, chifforobe, chair, desk and bedside table. "This is perfect."

"Glad you like it. The only meal I serve is Sunday dinner at one o'clock."

He walked to the window and peered down at the front yard. "Sounds good, I hope I'm in town for your meal this Sunday. By the way, I need a car. Is there any place in town where I can rent an automobile?"

"My husband works for Bartholomew Auto Sales, maybe he can help you. Ask for Avery Lester."

"Thank you." He made one more sweep of the room. He said his goodbyes to Ella and made his way down the walk to the waiting taxicab. "Charles, take me to Bartholomew Auto Sales."

"Sure thing."

He stared out the side window of the taxicab memorizing roads and signs, so he could find his way back to his rented room.

The car slowed and pulled into a gravel lot filled with automobiles. "Here we are, want me to wait for you?"

He pulled some money out of his pocket. "I hope they rent me a car. If they don't, I'll call you. Nice to meet you and thanks."

The cabbie took the money and stuffed the cash in his shirt pocket. "Good luck to ya."

A cream-colored nineteen thirty-eight Chevrolet sedan caught his eye. He walked around the car, opened the driver side door and peered in.

A man walked toward him, hand stuck out in greeting. "Avery Lester. You've got good taste, that's a fine automobile."

He returned the firm handshake. "Paul Williams and you're the man I'm looking for. I'm renting a room at your wife's boarding house and she said you might rent me a car."

Avery tilted his head. "We sell cars."

"I work as an airplane salesman out of Wichita, Kansas. I need something to get me from Andrews Field to town a few days a week. I'll travel by air the rest of the time." He ran his hand over the hood of the car.

"Andrews Field? I guess you met my son-in-law." Avery opened the hood.

"Yes, he's going to lease me a space for an office." Both men stared at the engine. "Maybe you could inquire about a car for me?"

Avery closed the hood and removed a rag from his pocket to clean his hands. He used the rag to wipe smudges off the car. "Come in, I'll ask Mr. Bartholomew if he'll rent you something. How long will you need it?"

"Six months to a year while I cover the airports in the Southeast."

Avery held the door open and let him enter. "Wait here, I'll be right back."

He glanced around the small office and waited while his new friend talked to an older balding gentleman. The man shook his head, but the car salesman persisted. The owner wrote something on a piece of paper. Avery studied the note and nodded.

Mr. Lester walked toward him with a spring in his step and a smile on his face. He gave Paul the missive. "Mr. Bartholomew doesn't rent cars but he's making an exception. He said he'd rent the Chevrolet for this amount due the first of each month."

He ran figures in his head. "That's fair, I'll take it."

"Have a seat, and we'll get the paperwork started." Avery nodded to a desk.

He signed the papers and handed over the money

for the month.

The salesman opened a desk drawer and pulled out a key. "Here you go, key to the Chevrolet sedan and welcome to Saplingville."

He stood, put the key in his left hand and shook the salesman's hand with his right. "Thank you, pleasure doing business."

Avery smiled. "Pleasure was all mine."

He headed toward the door, stopped and walked back to the desk. "Hey, do you have a map of the town?"

"Sure do." The older man opened a side drawer. "Here you go." He passed the map to the airplane salesman. "The town's easy to figure out but take care on the country roads, some aren't marked, and you could end up in the next county."

"Thanks, I'll get lunch somewhere and study this map before I head back to Andrews Field."

Avery walked him to the door. "Good idea. The bus station serves the best lunch, if you like good ol' southern food. They've got the best pinto beans and cornbread in town. Good luck to you."

He opened his hand showing the key. "Thanks again."

Paul made another pass down Main Street before he found the bus station. He arrived right before a bus headed for Savannah unloaded passengers for lunch. He grabbed a tray and made his way down the lunch line. The aromas from the various vegetables and meats made his stomach growl. He ordered fried chicken, pinto beans, coleslaw and cornbread. A heap of green and brown small medallions caught his eye. "What is that?" He asked the lady server.

"This is fried okra; it's abundant in the South. I can tell by your accent you aren't from these parts." She put a couple of pieces of okra in a spoon. "It's slimy boiled but fried it's delicious. Have a taste."

He took the spoon and savored the cornmeal-battered vegetable. "Very good, I'll have a bowl of the okra, also." He waited in line for his turn to pay.

The attendant handed him a glass of liquid with a lemon stuck in the rim. "Tea comes with your meal."

"Thank you." He pulled out his money clip and paid the man.

He sat at a table next to the window, so he could observe the people. He drank a sip of tea, the drink was sweet and cold, what he needed on a hot day. He cut a piece of chicken with his knife and fork. The skin was crunchy and the white meat moist. The thick soup of the pinto beans clung to his fork and the coleslaw was crisp and cold. Other diners picked their chicken up with their hands, so he did the same and abandoned the fork. The cornbread, something he didn't have at home, had a crusty brown exterior but moist and soft on the inside. The okra crunchy but tender was the best part of the meal. Everything was lip-smacking good, as they say in the South.

He finished his lunch and opened the map. He studied the layout of Saplingville and noted the road to the airport. Various conversations floated around him. He would arrive in Savannah long before these people. His thoughts drifted to Lisbeth. Her blue eyes and fiery personality haunted him. He wanted to discover what made her decide to become a pilot and female mechanic. He'd met female aviators; Amelia Earhart and Louise Thaden were his father's friends. The disappearance of Earhart and her airplane two years ago had filled the newspapers. More speculation than fact.

He folded the map and left the noisy restaurant. He rolled all the windows in the car down and headed out of town to Andrews Field studying every road sign and landmark he passed. In his mind he pictured the town from the air, memorizing how the streets ran parallel and in squares.

He turned his car into the parking lot of the small airport. An old bi-plane, a Curtiss JN-Four model, sat in front of the hangar. Lisbeth stood on a ladder with her head in the engine. He got out of his car and joined them. "Haven't seen one of these in a long time."

Frankie wiped his hands on a rag. "Yep, this is the Jenny I flew with the barnstormer team. It's stored in a shed next to the pasture."

A hot summer day at an airfield flashed through his mind. "Frankie Howard, now I remember. My dad and I went to a flying circus when I was a kid. You were billed as the youngest and best barnstormer ever. This is a real pleasure meeting you and seeing the very airplane you flew back then."

He deflected the comment with laughter. "I was young all right and not smart enough to be scared. I had a good time, though. The old Jenny still flies good; you'll have to take her up."

He examined the plane. "I've never flown one of these." He gave Lisbeth a knowing smile. "I bet you've flown the bi-plane."

She walked toward him. "Why'd you say that?"

He looked into her blue eyes, and a spark ignited in his belly. "Doesn't appear you're scared of anything. I bet you even do tricks."

She grabbed a spark plug and headed back to the engine. "Frankie taught me a few aerobatics."

He stared as she went about the business of servicing the Jenny. He wanted to pull her cap off and see if she had long hair.

The silence lengthened until the barnstormer said, "So, you're flying to Savannah today?"

He continued to watch the woman, amazed at her abilities. "Yes, want to go up with me for a quick flight through town? I need to study the roads from the sky, you can show me landmarks." He turned his attention to Frankie.

"If you have time, I'd love to fly in that plane." Frankie wiped his hands on a rag.

She dipped her fingers in grease to apply to the valve gear. "Want to go up, Lisbeth?" He cringed at the nasty lubricant covering her hands.

She continued her work. "No, thanks."

They walked toward the airplane. Paul opened the door and they gazed in the cabin. "I think I pissed her off."

Frankie climbed into the co-pilot's seat. "She doesn't take kindly to criticism. She's good and she knows it. Smartest woman I ever met."

He settled into his seat and checked his list. "I hear you're married to her sister."

The barnstormer laughed. "I am. She's as stubborn and bull-headed as Lisbeth."

"What about Al, is he family?" He fastened his seatbelt.

Frankie stared at the gauges and placed his hands on the wheel. "Yeah, Al's family, but not blood. He's been more of a father to me than my old man was."

They stayed in the air for thirty minutes. He focused on the streets and listened as the man pointed out the location of houses and businesses in town. He studied the city from the air. "I know how to get around now. Studying the map and seeing the roads from the sky make it clear."

Frankie pointed out his house in town. "We're having a birthday party for my son Saturday night. He's turning one. If you're in town, we'd enjoy having you."

He stared at the little house, not much bigger than the shed their gardener kept his tools in. "Thanks, I'm happy to attend." A grin filled his face and excitement bubbled in his belly. He liked this town and the people. A blue-eyed lady flyer was the icing on the cake.

Chapter Three

Lisbeth instructed her Friday afternoon student to check the compass and head south to the air strip. As they approached Andrews Field, she recognized the Twin Beech parked to the side of the runway. Excitement gnawed at her stomach while a compulsion to see Paul again spurred her to take command. She turned her attention to the student. "Taking control, I'll land."

She landed the plane and taxied to a tie-down spot. "Good job today, next week we'll work only on take-offs and landings. I think you're ready."

She shook the man's hand and ventured toward the hangar. A guffaw of laughter welcomed her. The men trying to one up each other with blond jokes didn't hear her come in.

Frankie's voice boomed through the hangar. "That was a good one, but I've got one better."

Al nudged him and turned his head toward her desk.

Victor spotted her and changed the subject. "Tell us about your trip to Savannah, sell any planes?"

She ignored them and finished her notes. She filed the paperwork in the student's notebook and placed it in the bookcase. She pulled a book from the shelf and sat at her desk to study. She cut her eyes toward the men. Paul's intense stare directed at her brought discomfort, but she presented him with a stare of her own then pretended to read.

The two men went back to their duties while Paul talked to Victor for another fifteen minutes. Her ears focused on his voice while her eyes scanned the pages. The conversation ended and he walked toward her.

The salesman stood at her desk and addressed her. "Lisbeth?"

She dog-eared the page and closed the book. "You need something?"

"I think we got off on the wrong foot. If I said anything to upset you, I'm sorry." He pulled up a chair and sat.

She wanted to believe him, but she'd been down this road before. Men said what they thought you wanted to hear to your face and another thing behind your back. "I'm not upset...you'd know if I was."

"I'm sure I would." He picked up the picture of Amelia Earhart. "You met her?"

She nodded. "A month before she..."

He placed the picture on the desk. "I knew her. My parents had her and Louise Thaden over for dinner right after the Women's Air Race in nineteen twenty-nine. It was a long time ago. I was thirteen."

"Your parents are aviators?"

"My father's a pilot for Trans World Airlines. Mother died three years ago." He stared at the floor. "Cancer."

The pain in his voice made her realize he was human. "I'm very sorry."

"Thank you." He picked up her book and read the title on the spine. "*Mechanical Engineering for Aviators*? I've got lots of books on mechanical engineering if you'd like to borrow them."

She studied his face, trying to read if he was sincere or patronizing her. "That's kind of you."

"Enjoyed talking to you, I've got some paperwork to finish." He headed to his desk.

She stared as he walked away. Even from the back he appeared handsome in his tailored trousers. He had his sleeves rolled up to the elbows. She'd noticed his arms when he picked up the picture frame. His skin appeared smooth and flawless. She supposed touching his flesh would feel like her velvet evening purse. She ascertained he came from a family with money and if naked without his fancy clothes would still have a rich look about him. She was jealous of his confidence and his way with people. Frankie, Victor, and Al hung on his every word. That's all the men talked about this week. Paul and his airplane, Paul and his job with Beech Aircraft Company, Paul and his freedom to fly around the country.

He made a phone call and readied his paper and pencil. "Mr. Reynolds, please. Paul Williams calling."

She tried not to listen as he recounted his week to his boss, but their desks located close together let her hear every word. He'd sold a Twin Beech to an airport in Savannah and they wanted delivery as soon as possible. He wrote something on his paper. "Got it, I'll get in touch with his secretary and set up a meeting in Atlanta next week." She listened closer when he mentioned Cessna Aircraft. "No, I don't think he'll be interested in a Cessna. Yes, I know our competition. I'll make sure he knows the benefits of owning a Beech."

She pulled a letter from her desk drawer dated one month ago from Beech Aircraft Company. She'd memorized the letter and her eyes fell to the last sentence. *Thank you for your interest in the test pilot job but the position has already been filled.* It was what the letter didn't say that made her angry. The letter didn't say they wouldn't consider her for the position because she was a woman. She hoped Beech would take her into account since they sponsored Louise Thaden in the Women's Air Derby of nineteen twenty-nine and she won flying a Travel Air. Of course, they wouldn't acknowledge her; she was a nobody from a little town in the South.

She put the letter in the top desk drawer, pulled out her flying magazine, and found the ad Cessna placed for test pilots, both companies located in Wichita, Kansas. She dreamed of working as a test pilot and flying the new ships before anyone else did. It was a lofty goal for a girl from a little Georgia town and she didn't cotton to anyone telling her she couldn't do it, so she'd kept her dream hidden. She mailed Cessna a letter last week but hadn't heard from them.

She placed the magazine in the top drawer of her desk and wandered to her brother's office. "I'm going to fly the Airmaster and check out my work. We told Mr. Spangler the repairs would be done today."

Victor put some papers in a drawer and stood. "I'll go with you."

She readied the plane and climbed in the pilot seat.

Her brother did his co-pilot duty and checked off the pre-flight list. "Any problems repairing the engine?" He fastened his seatbelt.

"None at all." She stared out the window as Paul ran toward the plane flailing his arms. "What does he want?"

She opened the airplane door. "Did you need something?" Her eyes locked with his. It seemed like an eternity while she waited for him to speak. Something stirred deep inside her core. She broke eye contact, and looked over his head, avoiding his eyes.

He gave her a heart-melting grin. "If you're doing a test flight, I'd like to join you."

She remembered his scathing words about her abilities. "Are you sure? I repaired this plane, but it hasn't been given the men's stamp of approval yet."

His face split into a wide grin. "Yeah, I deserved that. Sorry for what I said. Sometimes my mouth gets ahead of my brain. I told you I knew Miss Earhart and Miss Thaden, but I've never met an ordinary woman who repairs and flies airplanes."

Lisbeth's voice screeched. She'd love to punch his lights out. "Ordinary woman?"

He stared at the sky and let a puff of air escape his lungs. "Guess I did it again. I didn't mean you are unremarkable or commonplace. You're…"

"Go around. Victor will let you in on his side." She halted his explanation.

She listened for the click of his seatbelt before she taxied down the runway. She made sure she did a perfect take-off and prayed she'd nail the landing.

Her brother turned his head toward the back of the plane. "This Cessna belongs to Mr. Spangler. He owns the cotton mill in town. Funny story. When Frankie came back to town after working on the Barnstormer team, he got a job at the mill. He hated working there but he did his best and was promoted to Assistant Day Supervisor. A month after he received his new job, I opened the airport and he came to work for me. Mr.

Spangler became fascinated with airplanes and came out every Sunday for a ride in the Tri-Motor. Frankie gave him flying lessons and he bought this Cessna. He keeps the airplane on his farm a few miles from here."

He nodded. "You know, when Malcolm Reynolds told me about your setup and how close you are to the big cities of the South, I assumed I'd deal with a bunch of ignorant hicks in the middle of nowhere. I'm pleasantly surprised."

Heat scorched her face. Everything this man said infuriated her. "You're surprised, huh?"

He studied her profile. "Gee, I'm sorry. All I do is put my foot in my mouth. I'm trying to tell you how impressed I am with your operation here and with all of you."

"We understand what you mean." Victor acknowledged his sister and nodded his head. "Fly over town and show Paul where we live."

He peered out the window at the small town. "Frankie showed me his house. Do you live far from him?"

Victor pointed out the steeple on New Hope Baptist Church. "We all live in walking distance of the church. The house with the nineteen thirty-two black Buick in the yard is where Lisbeth lives with our parents."

He peered at the dwelling. "Nice house."

She turned the plane toward her brother's home.

"The two-story on the corner belongs to me and Dottie." Victor beamed.

Paul said. "Very nice. The layout of the streets makes places easy to find."

She turned the plane in the direction of Andrews

Field. She concentrated on flying and listened while the men made small talk. Paul said he lived with his father in Wichita, Kansas in a large house. A married couple worked for them and lived in a cottage behind his home for the last twenty years. The lady was the housekeeper and cook and the husband did house maintenance and gardening.

So her suspicions were correct. He was from money. She wondered what her mother would think about a cook and housekeeper running her house. She couldn't imagine Hattie Douglas relinquishing any of her duties to someone else. The airfield loomed ahead. Even though she'd landed hundreds of times, she heard Frankie's voice in her head instructing her. The landing was smooth just like he'd taught her. She unfastened her safety belt, turned in her seat, and gave Paul a self-assured grin.

"Damn. You're good." He winked and captured her eyes with a wicked grin.

"Thank you." She didn't want to leave the plane, she wanted to sit and stare into his eyes, but Victor was already out waiting for them. They exited the plane. The men started a conversation, so she strolled to the hangar.

Frankie put his notepad in his drawer. "Any problems with Mr. Spangler's airplane?"

She continued walking. "None. I'll call his secretary, so she can let him know it's ready."

"You coming to Jake's birthday party tomorrow night?"

Lisbeth smiled at the memory of the little red-haired baby that had stolen her heart. "Wouldn't miss it."

Her brother-in-law grabbed his car keys. "Hey, Al, you and Ethel coming to the party?"

Al put his broom in the closet. "Of course. Wouldn't miss the little feller turnin' one."

Frankie walked toward the door. "See ya'll tomorrow night."

Al approached her desk. "I see you let Paul go up with you."

She gazed at the old man and bit her lip. She stared at him for a minute, waiting for the advice she knew was coming. "He said he wanted to come with us and see where we lived in town."

He stared at her and smiled. "Don't be hard on him. He's a Yankee."

She chuckled, "He's from the Midwest."

"Midwest, Yankee, same thing. He's a good man, I can tell. He's a little different from us South'ners."

"He's from a rich family and has a college education and is quite a jerk when he wants to be."

He shook his head and made a clicking sound with his tongue. "See what I mean, you're talking about him and he's not here to defend himself. You could have a college education, but you chose flying and most people in town believe you came from money. It's all about the perspective."

She picked up the phone to signal the conversation was over. "I need to call Mr. Spangler. See you tomorrow, Al."

"See you, Missy." Al hesitated and gave her a smile before he turned for the door.

Cecelia, Mr. Spangler's secretary, assured her she'd relay the message. She leaned back in her chair and reflected on Al's words. She hated to admit it, but

Al was usually right. He had a sixth sense about people. He could read you like a book. The quiet man kept to himself but didn't miss a thing that went on in the hangar. She grabbed her car keys. Her ma's supper and a hot bath called her name.

Chapter Four

Paul and Victor stood in the shade of the awning outside the hangar door. He gave the airport owner his spiel intent on selling a Twin Beech when Lisbeth came out the door and walked to her car. He lost his words when she gave them a wave and climbed in her dark blue nineteen thirty-three Chevrolet Coupe. The car was sporty and pretty like her. He looked forward to the party, couldn't wait to see her out of her coveralls and hat. Surely, she didn't dress like a mechanic all the time. He reeled his attention back to the conversation.

Victor shoved his hands in his pockets. "I would like nothing more than to buy the airplane, but I can't afford to spend that kind of money until I have the Tri-Motor paid for next year."

Lisbeth's car pulled out onto the road and he listened as she changed gears and sped away. "Sure, I understand. Give us Beech people a chance before the Cessna folks is all I ask."

"Of course. You know we love the Beech Staggerwing. Great plane."

Ready to leave, he shook the man's hand. "Thanks. See you guys tomorrow night." He entered the building and strolled to his space. He grabbed his coat and briefcase from his desk. The quietness of the hangar with everyone gone for the day quickened his step.

He put his personal items on the passenger side and

rolled down the window before he walked around the car to the driver's side. He removed his shirt and placed it in the back seat before getting in the car. He never wore a T-shirt out in public, but he'd seen plenty of men in town dressed casually. His mother wouldn't approve, but then she'd never lived in the heat and humidity of the South. With the windows down hot air flowed through the car. The scenery was nice, and he loved the hills and trees better than the flat lands of the Midwest. He drove by a small house with a large cotton patch. A man, woman, and three young boys hoed a crop of cotton; he realized how hot they were in the scorching sun and reprimanded himself for complaining.

****

Paul spent his Saturday at the desk in his room filling out paperwork for his first sale. The desk in front of one of the windows gave him a view into the street where people wandered along the sidewalk. Kids kicked a ball and chased each other; the sights and sounds were foreign. He grew up in a large house on ten acres with no neighbors.

The people of the South went out of their way to wave if you drove by and stopped to talk when they encountered you on the street. He noticed under their polite demeanor was a thread of proud toughness. The shanty village on the edge of town and the shells of buildings closed due to the Wall Street crash of nineteen twenty-nine stood as a constant reminder of what happened and could happen again. These people refused to let their guard down. He had a long row to hoe selling airplanes in the South; he was grateful the first week proved productive.

He put away his work and opened the chifforobe. He decided on a pair of gray trousers, white shirt, striped tie, and suspenders. He grabbed the small wooden bi-plane he found at the dime store and walked downstairs. The house was quiet; a boarder sat on the settee reading a book. He opened the screen door and closed it gently, not wanting to disturb the gentleman, plus he didn't enjoy the slap of the screen door he'd heard too many times today to count.

He arrived at Frankie's house and noticed several cars parked along the street. He recognized Al's old truck and parked behind the Chevrolet. As he walked toward the small house, he heard talking and laughing. His parents made sure he knew how to interact in social situations with important, influential people, but they didn't teach him how to fit in with the ordinary crowd.

He knocked on the door and a pretty dark-haired young woman greeted him. "Hi, you must be Paul. I'm Ruth Ann, Frankie's wife. Please, come in."

He entered the house and surveyed the small room filled with people. A little red-haired baby toddled toward him, grabbed his leg, held on with one hand and waved the other in the air. "Pane, Pane."

Paul didn't move, afraid the tyke would fall.

Frankie scooped up the baby and put him on his shoulder. Jake reached for the wooden airplane. "This is Jacob Albert Howard. We call him Jake. He likes the wooden bi-plane you're holding."

He handed the plane to the baby. "Happy birthday, Jake."

The baby boy grabbed the wooden toy and raised it over his head. "Pane, Pane."

The father beamed with pride. "He's trying to say

'plane.' Believe it or not, that was the first word he learned."

He admired the baby boy, so much like his father already. "With you for a daddy, I'd be very surprised if it wasn't his first word."

He spotted two children standing to the side. He put his hands on his knees and bent down giving them a smile. "Who are these two cuties?"

Frankie turned and motioned to them. "Come over here and meet Mr. Williams. He works at the hangar with us."

The little boy grabbed his sister's hand and pulled her toward him.

Their uncle nudged them forward. "These little fellows belong to Victor and Dottie; they're twins. Jack Andrew and Carol Ann, say hello to Mr. Williams."

He crouched on his knees. "It's nice to meet you, Jack Andrew and Carol Ann."

The kids giggled, turned, and ran to their mother.

He rose to his full height and searched the room; only one person was on his mind. He wondered if he would recognize her out of her work clothes.

At that moment, she entered the living room from the kitchen. His heart raced at the vision of her. Her dark hair surrounded her shoulders and upper back while bangs framed her blue eyes. She wore a white blouse with a cameo pin centered at the base of her neck. He eyed her curvy bosom, the small waist of her navy skirt, and her perfect legs. Never in his mind could he imagine the beauty before him. He cleared his throat and attempted to form a word. "Lisbeth."

She grinned and walked toward him. "Paul, good to see you. I think you know everyone except my parents, my aunt and uncle, and Al's lady friend."

Jacob, Hattie, Walter, Delores and Ethel approached him.

He gave the men each a firm handshake and kissed Hattie's, Dolores', and Ethel's hands. "Nice to meet you."

Her mother giggled like a school girl. "So nice to meet you. We're glad you could join us for Jake's first birthday."

"Well, I'm honored Frankie asked me."

She started firing questions at him about where he was from and how long he would live in Saplingville.

Delores took her arm and pulled her toward the kitchen. "Come on, Hattie, let's get the food ready. There's plenty of time to talk later."

Lisbeth stood next to him and whispered, "Sorry, she's kind of pushy and nosy."

He nodded. "My mother too, but she was discreet. She'd get it out of you before you knew you told her. The aroma coming from the kitchen is amazing. What's that wonderful smell?"

"Barbeque. Walter and Delores smoked some pork and Ma brought baked beans and potato salad."

He turned his attention to the beauty before him. "One thing I can say about you southern people. You sure have some good food around here."

"I would think someone with a cook living in their house would have the best." She guided him toward the front of the room, out of eyesight from her mother's prying eyes.

"Yes, she's an excellent cook, but the taste is different. It's plainer, not seasoned as much, and we don't have the variety of vegetables you have here. I didn't know what okra was until I ate it for lunch at the bus station."

Frankie grabbed his son and whistled to get everyone's attention. He held Jake in one arm and put his other around Ruth Ann. "Thank y'all for coming to Jake's birthday party. You're the best family this country boy could hope for. If you will kindly bow your heads, I'll say the blessing."

Paul stood back, but everyone insisted he fix his plate first. No one would follow him until Lisbeth stepped up. He scooped a little from each bowl until his plate was full.

She handed him a glass of sweet tea. "Here, take this and we'll eat outside."

He followed her to the porch and waited for her to sit on the bench before he sat down. The night was getting better and better. He set his tea on the armrest and took a bite of barbecue. He closed his eyes and savored the taste. Sweet, salty, spicy, smoky and the meat so tender it melted in his mouth. "Wow, this is good."

She dipped a piece of bread in the tangy sauce and raised it to his mouth. "Try this."

He took the bite, tempted to suck her finger into his mouth along with the bread. "Amazing. We have barbecue in Kansas but it's different. Our sauce is thicker and sweeter."

He mounded his fork with baked beans. A smoky molasses taste teased his tongue. "They're sweet but have a tart flavor."

"That's the mustard playing off the brown sugar." Lisbeth wiped her mouth with the cloth napkin. "How do you like the potato salad?"

"Delicious. What's the crunchy part?" He examined the salad on his fork.

"Ma puts a little cut up apple in her potato salad. Good, huh?"

"Delicious." He cut a piece of meat with his knife. "Do you cook as good as your ma?"

"She taught Ruth Ann and me as soon as we could reach the kitchen counter. We always helped in the kitchen. I made the potato salad."

"Well, it's the best I've ever had." Her smile made him want to taste something other than the potato salad. "I've been meaning to ask you. Is Lisbeth short for Elizabeth?"

"No, I was named Lisbeth Rose. Rose was my grandmother's name." She took a sip of tea.

"A beautiful name for a beautiful woman." Gazing into her eyes heat rushed through his body and settled in his groin. He raised her chin to face him and planted a gentle kiss on her mouth. The tender touch of her lips and the innocent smile on her face seized his heart.

"And what is your full name?"

Captivated by her eyes, he had to remind himself what his name was. "Paul Louis."

She grinned and continued eating. "That's a nice name, too."

"What do you do for fun around here?" He finished off his plate of food and drank the remainder of his iced tea.

She stacked their plates on the end table. "We have the movie theater, but most of our lives revolve around the church socials and gatherings. Do you attend a church in Wichita?"

He held her hand and turned it over, amazed the

grease from the airplane engine was gone and only a rough patch of skin remained on her index finger. "Yes, First Presbyterian."

She reached for the plates and stood. "Let's go in and see if they're ready to cut the birthday cake."

He retrieved their glasses and followed her in the house.

Frankie had Jake perched on his shoulders while the family sang "Happy Birthday." Ruth Ann passed out slices of cake while Hattie poured coffee in cups.

After dessert, Paul made his way around the room, thanking each person for the lovely evening and delicious food. Lisbeth walked him out to the porch and watched as he cranked his car and drove off. He liked Lisbeth Rose, but his father wouldn't. Matthew Williams wanted his son to marry one of the rich girls from home. He and Marjorie had made sure their son mingled with the top society of Wichita and encouraged him to date a debutante. He resented it, dated girls they wouldn't approve of, and brought them home for the weekend as an act of rebellion. Lisbeth could see through bullshit; she would never let anyone use her. He had to tread carefully with this one.

Chapter Five

Lisbeth opened her eyes and stared outside her window as the sunrise illuminated the tree next to the house. She stretched and turned on her back staring up at the ceiling. Sleep didn't come until after midnight, the excitement from her evening with Paul and their stolen kiss had her body wound like a bobbin in her mother's Singer sewing machine. Her body heated from the memory and her core tingled as it begged for release. She turned on her side and imagined him lying beside her, holding her close. She fantasized about how he lived in Wichita with his rich father, servants and a huge house. She'd never fit in that life. However, he was now living in a small room at the boarding house and he seemed comfortable at the party last night.

She pulled on her robe and walked down the stairs to the parlor.

Jacob sat in his chair, reading the front page of the morning paper. "You're up early."

"Couldn't sleep." She grabbed the business section and settled on the sofa.

He put his paper down. "I'm glad you're up, I wanted to talk to you."

A sinking feeling filled her belly. Ever since his heart attack she'd been terrified he would have another. "Is something wrong? You aren't sick, are you?"

He smiled. "No, never better. I'm worried about

you. All I see is you working long hours and come in at night tired, greased up like a pig. On Saturday mornings you teach piano at Ruth Ann's studio, play at church on Sunday and take people for rides most Sunday afternoons. I haven't seen you go out with your friends in a long time. Even I close the drug store on Sundays and take a day off work to rest."

"Pa, you know I love all my jobs especially flying. Besides, most of my girlfriends are married. We have nothing in common anymore. I enjoy teaching piano and playing at church. I'm fortunate that I love everything I do, and nothing seems like work."

Her father picked up the mechanical engineering book and thumbed through the pages. "Interesting books you've been studying." He returned the book to the table. "I hope you don't mind, I've been reading them myself."

"Of course not." She avoided eye contact with her father and weighed the pros and cons of telling him the truth.

He continued. "It's not too late for you to go to college and become an engineer. I'm proud of you and want you to have every opportunity."

Is this the time to tell her father her lofty goal? She studied the hardwood floor and struggled with her decision. What if he didn't approve or worse tell her she would never have the skills? "Pa, there is a job I've been considering."

Jacob stared at his daughter. "What is that?"

She bit her lower lip and wondered if she dare say the words aloud. "I want to work as a test pilot."

He turned his ear toward her. "Did you say test pilot?"

She scooted to the end of the sofa closer to her father's chair. "Yes, Cessna Aircraft Company is hiring."

He closed his eyes and rubbed his head with his hand.

She stared at her father, waiting for him to say something.

Minutes passed before he responded. "A test pilot?"

She nodded.

"Where is Cessna Aircraft located?"

"Wichita, Kansas."

"That's a long way from Saplingville, Georgia."

"I know, Pa."

Jacob settled in his seat, rested his head on the back of the chair and closed his eyes.

She reached for her father's hand. "I'm sorry Pa, I don't want you to worry but I need to do this."

He looked into his youngest daughter's eyes and nodded his head. "I don't like this idea, but I understand. There's a place in life for everyone. Some people are happy with their lot in a small town. They find their place and make a contribution to society. You're destined for great things and I know nothing I say will stop you. Please make safety first priority and don't take chances, is all I ask."

She hugged her father. "Thanks, Pa. I promise to always put safety first and never take short cuts and chances. I learned from the best pilots in the world right here in Saplingville. They drilled the mantra into my head from the start of my training."

"Have you applied?"

"Yes." She couldn't tell him she'd already been

turned down by Beech Aircraft Company. Her disappointment still fresh, she feared she'd cry.

"You're a good daughter. I appreciate your trust in me."

She gave her pa a big smile, their gazes locked. She had a connection with him. Most of the time they knew what the other was thinking without saying the words. She got along with her mother as well as oil and water mixed together. Hattie was easier on her than Ruth Ann, but Lisbeth didn't rebel and cause trouble like her sister had before she married Frankie.

"Pa, can we keep this between us?"

"For now." Jacob picked up the newspaper and continued reading.

****

Pastor Lowe stood at the podium welcoming everyone to the Sunday service when Paul entered the church and sat in the back row. Lisbeth's hands became wet with perspiration while the nerve endings in her body came to life. She'd played the piano at church since she was thirteen. She'd seen her share of train wrecks, lights going off at night services and playing by oil lamp, singers who forgot their words or sang off key, losing her place on the page, and music flying off the piano when a strong wind swept through the church on hot Sunday mornings. None of this ever fazed her. Paul Williams attending the service this morning put her over the edge. Every pew overflowed with people, how could one person make her this nervous?

Victor stepped to the podium and announced the first song. She sucked a deep breath into her lungs and said a prayer. She played three wrong notes in the introduction. Her brother turned his head and stared.

She ignored him and continued. He brought the congregation in at the right moment. She pressed the soft pedal of the piano to mute any other mistakes she might make. When the song was over, she decided he knew how bad she played so whatever she did during the rest of the service didn't matter. The realization calmed her so she could continue.

At the end of the service, the pastor stood in front of the pews begging people to come to the Lord while she played 'Just As I Am' softly on the piano. She stared into the congregation at no one in particular when Paul made his way out of the church.

****

Jacob listened to the radio while his wife and Lisbeth prepared Sunday Dinner.

Hattie opened a jar of home canned green beans and rinsed them. "What do you know about this Paul Williams?"

Lisbeth cracked an egg and dumped it in a bowl of cornmeal, added buttermilk and stirred. "I know he's working for Beech Aircraft Company and Victor rents him a space at the hangar."

"Where's he from?"

"Wichita, Kansas."

Ma added a small amount of water to the green beans along with a spoonful of bacon grease from the can on the counter, sprinkled salt and pepper over the beans and positioned the pan on the stove eye. "You were getting chummy with him last night. Do you like him?"

Lisbeth poured oil into the iron skillet to heat. "We just met, I don't know him enough to know if I like him or not."

Her mother grabbed the pot holders and placed the hot pan of roast beef on a medal trivet. "He's a handsome boy; I wish he was from around here. I don't want you moving to Kansas."

She watched the oil in the skillet, waiting until it was hot to pour into the mix. Her mother would forgive her if she moved to another city because of marriage but leaving Saplingville for a job, one she knew her mother would not approve of was another story. She needed to keep her in the dark as long as possible. "Ma, stop trying to find me a husband."

Hattie moved to the stove and stared at the hot oil. "You're gonna set the house on fire if you don't pour the oil in the cornbread batter right now."

Lisbeth poured the hot oil in the mix and stirred. She poured the mixture into the hot iron skillet and slid it in the oven.

Her mother handed her plates for the table. "He's very handsome, maybe he'll decide to move to Saplingville."

She placed the plates on the table and rolled her eyes. "Ma, please."

"Well, he's handsome and he was paying close attention to you last night. Couldn't take his eyes off you." Her mother pulled some cloth napkins out of a drawer.

He'd stared; his eyes raked over her before he flashed her a smile that caused her heart to race. She did look better in her skirt and blouse than her greasy coveralls, she hoped.

Hattie set the bowls of food on the table and stuck her head in the parlor door. "Food's ready."

Jacob washed his hands at the kitchen sink.

"Smells good. You always outdo yourself Henrietta." He sat at the table and said a blessing over the food.

"I was telling Lisbeth what a nice young gentleman Paul seemed to be." She passed the green beans to her husband.

He scooped the vegetable and placed a spoon full on his plate. "Yes, he seems like a nice fellow."

"I told her he could move to Saplingville if they got married. Victor could give him a job. We don't want our daughter leaving us."

He passed Lisbeth the bowl of beans and stared into her eyes as he spoke to his wife. "Henrietta, she's grown now, we have to let her make her own choices. The man hasn't even asked her out."

"He will. He's smitten, I just know it." She poured gravy on her pot roast.

Lisbeth put her fork down. "I'm sitting here, Ma. I hear everything you're saying. Stop talking about me like I'm not."

"I'm sorry, honey. It's time for you to find someone and build a home and future. There aren't many nice boys left in town. He's the first prospect I've seen in a while."

A fury roared inside her only her mother could ignite. To keep from getting into a fight, she changed the subject. "I need to leave at two o'clock. It's my Sunday to fly the Tri-Motor."

"How's that going? Still have many customers?" Jacob smeared butter on his cornbread.

She smiled and nodded to her father, happy he'd changed the subject. "Fifteen people paid for a ride last week. Victor's pleased, he says if we continue to have at least fifteen a Sunday he'll have the Tri-Motor paid off by next year."

"Be careful." Hattie squeezed a lemon wedge into her tea.

"Always." She humored her mother with a smile.

"Smart move by Frankie convincing Victor to sell airplane rides." Jacob sliced his roast. "Tender meat; is this the beef we bought from Walter?"

"Yes, it is." Her ma replied. "Better than what we get from Simpson's Grocery."

Lisbeth helped herself to more green beans. "Frankie knew we would succeed from his experience flying with the barnstormers. He sold rides at every show they did and was allowed to pocket the money. He says a little overtime never hurt anybody and makes the worker richer."

Hattie walked to the counter and brought the pink glass cake plate to the table. "Frankie's the best son-in-law anyone could ask for. I want you to have someone good." She swapped their dinner plates for dessert plates. She cut into the Pineapple Upside Down Cake making sure everyone got a ring of pineapple with a cherry in the middle.

"I know, Ma." She glanced at the clock. "It's getting late. Save my piece for later." She kissed her father on the forehead. "I'll be home by six."

She started her car and headed toward Andrews Field. Paul was handsome, and he made her feel things no other man had. She didn't think he would ask her out. After all, he didn't even stay after church and say hello. He must have a beautiful rich debutante waiting in Wichita.

Chapter Six

Paul sat in the back of the Baptist Church and listened to Lisbeth play the piano. He could tell by the way she played the hymns she'd been classically trained. He didn't know Victor could sing. He glanced around; the few people he knew in this small town attended the church. So far this morning a woman stood up and said she wanted to testify. He didn't know what she meant until she recited the good things God had done for her.

After one of the songs a man stood up and shouted out a song request which Victor and Lisbeth turned their book to before the page was announced. Before the sermon, the minister asked the congregation for prayer requests. The congregation sought prayer for healing of ailments to rain and successful crops. During the sermon, Pastor Lowe raised his voice and slammed his hand on the podium.

The Presbyterian Church in Wichita was less animated and the service very structured. When the pastor gave an altar call, he decided to sneak out the door. He had a Christian upbringing and attended Sunday School and Vacation Bible School as a kid. His pastor never raised his voice during his sermon and made sure everyone understood the message.

This man screamed and pointed, and the people yelled, 'Amen.' He wondered if they spoke another language because he didn't understand much of what the preacher said. He couldn't lie to the man and tell him he enjoyed his sermon, so he left the church before anyone noticed he was there.

He walked to the boarding house and waited in the parlor for the food Ella had promised. The bookcase in the corner enticed him. He picked up "Magnificent Obsession" by Lloyd C. Douglas.

Avery entered the parlor. "Afternoon."

He placed the book on the shelf. "Good Afternoon. Lunch smells good."

"We call it Sunday Dinner in the South and yes, Ella's a fantastic cook. By the way, those books are for borrowing."

He put the book on top of the shelf; he planned to peruse it after lunch. "Thank you, I've always wanted to read this."

Ella walked from the kitchen holding a large brass bell. "Avery, call our friends, please."

Avery walked to the stairs; the loud tinkling of the bell filled the silence. "Don't know how many will eat lunch today. Do you like Fried Chicken?"

"I knew I smelled chicken frying this morning." He stood at the table and scanned the bowls of Chicken, Potato Salad, Green Beans, Cole Slaw and Juicy Red Tomatoes sliced in a plate.

Ella stepped into the dining room carrying a basket filled with bread. "Dottie taught me how to make her mother's biscuits, they're Avery's favorite."

"Dottie's a very nice lady. I got to know her at the hangar when she dropped by to see Victor."

Avery pointed to a chair. "Have a seat. She takes after her mother. My first wife died of cancer."

He sat in the chair. "My mom did, too. Horrible disease."

Three other boarders came in the room and Avery made introductions and said the blessing before passing around the bowls of food. "Paul, did you enjoy our Baptist Church? You left before I could welcome you."

Embarrassed he'd been found out, he responded. "I hoped no one would see me. I was late getting there and left before the service ended. I attend First Presbyterian in Wichita."

Avery nodded. "Different from what you're used to. Check out the Methodist Church next week, I think you'll like it better."

He appreciated Avery's diplomacy. "Thank you, I believe that's a better fit for me."

Paul ate seconds and didn't think he could eat another bite until Ella brought in the bowls of Peach Cobbler.

She circled the table filling tea glasses. "Anyone need anything else?"

He picked up his spoon and dug into his dessert. "Best food I've ever eaten. Thank you."

She sat down and filled her spoon with cobbler. "One of the perks of living at Ella's Boarding House."

He excused himself, left the table, picked up the book and went to his room. He got through a couple of chapters and glanced out the window. People strolled down the wide sidewalks. He laid the book on his desk and headed down the stairs. He stood at the door and hesitated, aware of his isolation in this strange town.

He gently opened and closed the screen door. This was another thing about the South. Every house had a screen door with the springs drawn tight, so the door snapped shut with a loud noise which got under his skin. He'd mentioned it to Avery, and he said that because of mosquitoes and flies, the door had to close quickly to keep as many out of the house as possible. He had enough of mosquitoes last night when he sat on the porch after dark. He'd rather endure Wichita's cold winters than the heat and humidity of the South with their infestation of mosquitoes and chiggers.

He wandered down Main Street and inspected the window displays. His eye was drawn to the Men's Store and the short sleeve shirts and summer pants on display. He made a mental note to check the place out in his spare time. The sound of airplane engines drew his gaze skyward. The Tri-Motor flew over. A banner streaming from the back of the plane proclaimed, "*Airplane Rides every Sunday at Andrews Field.*" He'd bet ten dollars Lisbeth sat at the controls.

****

Paul opened his eyes and rolled over in the bed. He tried to silence his alarm clock before he realized the ringing bell came from the Cotton Mill, most of the people in town worked there. They even had their own houses to live in which they called the mill village. When he went to sleep last night, the air was hot and stagnant and now the morning air was cool and brisk. He snuggled under the sheet, his body craved more sleep, but he had an important appointment in Atlanta. He dressed and prepared his suitcase for the week before heading to the Saplingville Diner for breakfast.

Joe and his wife Sally owned the restaurant. The food, too greasy for his taste, lay heavy in his stomach but as it was the only place open for breakfast, he became a regular.

Sally laughed at him when he put sugar and milk on his grits. She told him, "Oh my gawd, Mr. Williams, you ruint them grits." He'd given her a mind your own business expression daring her to say anything more. Now she brought him sugar and milk when he ordered grits and sat them on the table without a word.

The waitress stood at his table, pencil poised on her pad. A man at the next table poured red water on his bowl of grits. "What is the red liquid?"

She gave him a you've got to be kidding look. "Ain't you never seen red eye gravy before?"

He answered the woman. "No, I haven't."

"Well, red eye gravy is made by pouring coffee into ham grease. Your grits would taste better with some gravy on them instead of sugar…"

He raised his hand. "This morning, I'll have the bacon and egg sandwich and coffee, thank you." He tried okra and liked it, but he had to draw the line somewhere.

****

He turned in the parking lot of Andrews Field. The gang already on the job, he recognized each car. Victor had a good business and a stab of jealousy reared its head.

He entered the hangar and let his eyes adjust. Lisbeth perched atop a ladder with her head in an airplane engine. No surprise there. He walked toward her.

She acknowledged him. "Morning."

"Well, good morning to you. Did you take the Tri-Motor up yesterday?"

She climbed off the ladder. "Sure did. Frankie and I take turns flying people around town on Sunday afternoons."

He lowered his voice. "Hey, I'm leaving for the week but wanted to know if you'd have dinner with me Friday night. Is there a nice restaurant around here?"

"I'll go to dinner with you." She struggled to get the grease off her hands. "There's a good steak place next town over."

"That's where we'll go." Anticipation of a date with her caused his pants to tighten. He hoped she wouldn't notice.

She threw the greasy rag on the table. "Hope you have a good week and sell an airplane."

He looked into her blue eyes and lowered his head to give her a goodbye kiss until he remembered the crew could see them. "That's the plan." He spotted the janitor sweeping the floor trying to act like he was minding his own business, but Paul knew he heard every word. "Al, can you put gas in the Twin Beech for me?"

Al put his broom down and smiled. "Gotcha covered."

He moseyed to Victor's office. "Heading to Atlanta. See you guys at the end of the week."

"Not so fast, I heard on the radio a front's moving in. You should wait a few hours before flying out." The boss stood, tapping a pencil on his desk.

Paul rested his hands on the back of a chair. "Skies clear and blue. It's not far to Atlanta. I think it's better to leave now and get ahead of the storm. It's too late to reschedule my appointment."

"Whatever you think, wanted you to know a storm's brewing."

He hurried to his airplane and went through his

pre-flight checklist. The blue sky reminded him of Lisbeth's eyes. He made a smooth take-off and directed the plane toward Atlanta. Twenty minutes into his flight, the wind picked up. His eyes widened in horror as the dark clouds rolled toward the airplane. All at once, the Twin Beech rocked back and forth like a ship in a rough ocean. He pulled his seatbelt tighter and wiped the sweat off his forehead. His hands shook as he reduced the speed of the plane. All he could do was hold his reduced speed and ride it out. He couldn't fly above the clouds and he didn't know the terrain enough to fly below. Fear tore through his gut. Beads of sweat dropped from his face. He cursed himself for not standing up to his father. Matthew Williams wanted his son to work as a Trans World Airlines pilot like him. His dream lay in the design of airplanes. He had an engineering degree, for God's sake, what was he doing here?

The clouds opened, and a glimpse of blue sky peeked through the darkness. His body relaxed. He increased his speed and checked his compass to make sure he hadn't drifted off course. He would take Victor's advice next time…if there was a next time.

He landed at Candler Field and headed for the restaurant. He sat at the counter and ordered a cup of coffee.

The waitress smiled and poured coffee in a thick white mug. "You all right, sugar? Your face is as white as your starched shirt."

He read the woman's name tag, took the mug and spilled coffee on the counter. "Thanks Arlene. I came through a rough storm."

She wiped the hot liquid from the counter. "That

little thunderstorm? If that scared you, you need to find another business."

He drank a sip of coffee and held the mug in both hands. "I agree with you Arlene, but it's easier said than done."

She put the coffee pot down. "Ah, sugar, a good-looking man like you. You can be anything you want."

He ate a piece of apple pie and drank another cup of coffee before taking a taxi to the meeting with his client. He appreciated the waitress' advice and wished changing the course of his life was as easy as she said.

Chapter Seven

Lisbeth sat in her brother's office with Frankie. She drank a swig of cola from an ice-cold bottle. The fizzy drink bubbled up in her esophagus and she burped. Embarrassment heated her face while the men laughed at her. "Oh, my, I'm sorry. Please excuse me."

Victor smiled at his sister. "You're excused. I've got a list of things need doing this week and a customer called and wanted Frankie to fly them to Savannah this morning."

Frankie sat up straighter in his chair. "Sure can. Is it an overnighter?"

He put a check mark on his paper. "No, day trip, they're arriving within the hour. Lisbeth, finish the work on Mr. Johnston's Cessna. Frankie will fill you in on what else needs to be done."

She rolled the green glass bottle around in her hands. "No problem."

They walked toward the customer's plane while her brother-in-law explained what she needed to do to complete the job.

She worked for three hours on the engine. When she was satisfied with her work, she got a rag and cleaned the inside of the cockpit and windows. Al helped her push the plane from the hangar and she rinsed the exterior with the water hose. Mr. Johnston was their pickiest customer. He complained about everything, so she'd give the repairs and clean-up her best effort.

Finished with the job, she walked through the hangar to the office. "I've cleaned the Cessna inside and out. I'm taking it up for a test flight."

Victor talked on the phone. He put his hand over the mouthpiece. "Thanks."

She checked the engine and walked around the airplane, making notes on the checklist. Satisfied with the exterior, she settled in the pilot seat, completed the form, and placed the clipboard in the co-pilot seat. The engine fired on the first try, she paused and listened for any roughness, sputters or clicks. The Cessna lifted effortlessly into the cloudless blue sky headed for Saplingville. Happy with her work, she flew the plane back to Uncle Walter's farm and landed at Andrews Field.

Her elation from a job well done disappeared when she walked into the hanger to raised voices and angry shouts. She stared through the glass into the main office; her body trembled from the energy pouring from the two men.

Mr. Johnston stood with his fist in the air. "I told you when I brought my plane in, I wanted Frankie and only Frankie to repair it. I don't want some damned snotty nosed little girl touching my airplane."

Victor stood behind his desk with his hands on his hips. "He did most of the work on your plane. He was called out this morning to fly a customer to Savannah. Lisbeth finished what he started and checked out the work with a test flight."

The irate customer leaned over the desk. "I ought to damn sue you for ignoring my orders."

Victor folded his arms. "Lisbeth Douglas is a capable pilot and mechanic. She was trained by Frankie. Hell, she knows more about airplane engines than we do. If you don't like our work here, I suggest you find someone else to service your airplane."

"I'll do just that." The man stormed out of the office and came face to face with his adversary. He glared at her.

She presented him with her Bless Your Heart, Go to Hell smile. "Have a nice day, Mr. Johnston."

He stomped out of the hangar.

She wiped a tear from her face and sat in the chair in front of her brother's desk. "What an asshole. Did he pay you?"

He held up the check. "Yep."

She folded her hands in her lap and bit her bottom lip. The horrible words the customer said ravaged her brain and tears begged to escape her eyes. What started as a good day at work turned into a nightmare.

Victor put the check in his top drawer. "Better get this to the bank before he stops payment."

She apologized. "I'm sorry."

"It's not your fault, you said it yourself, he's an asshole. He complains about everything. I told him straight; find someone else to service your plane. I'm tired of trying to please the man."

"I did my best work, even cleaned the plane inside and out."

"I appreciate that. Don't let this man upset you."

"How many other customers have complained?"

He leaned back in his chair. "Just him, I promise. Take a break and eat your lunch, I'm going to town to run errands." Victor rummaged through the top drawer, stood and placed the check and ledger book in his briefcase. "I may not be back this afternoon, if I'm not, lock up, will you?"

"Sure." She dug a nickel from her pocket, pulled a cola from the cooler and took a long draw of the fizzy brown liquid. She settled in her desk chair and ate her tasteless sandwich while staring at the picture of Amelia Earhart. Days like this she remembered every word Amelia said. Their short meeting brief but filled with encouragement and praise from a woman who knew what challenges she would face. Hearing a man talk about her as Mr. Johnston had brought a new kind of doubt. All of her girlfriends married young, worked in a store in town or waited at home for their fiancé. She accepted the fact early on she'd rather work and fly than spend time with friends. She knew how they talked behind her back. They said she was stuck-up and assumed she was better than everyone. Truth be known, it was the opposite. How would they understand an airplane engine? Most of the people she knew wouldn't fly in an airplane. Her mother's words rode the tide into her brain. "Why can't you get married and settle down like your sister?" She whispered the words under her breath, "I may get married, but I'll never settle down."

Al sat across the hangar eating crackers and potted meat. "Did you say something?"

She shook her head. "No, nothing."

He smeared meat on his cracker with his pocket knife. "You all right?"

"Yeah, fine."

"You're a smart cookie. Don't let anyone tell you any different, you hear?"

"Thanks, Al."

She picked up her cola bottle and walked outside. She savored the cold liquid and gazed at the sky.

Al joined her. "Nice day today. I imagine Paul got to Atlanta with no problems yesterday and the storm weren't as bad close to Atlanta as here."

She watched the white clouds float through the blue sky. "I'm sure he's fine, we would have heard if something happened. He knows what he's doing."

"I hope so. He's too cocky for his own good."

She chuckled, thinking of his in-charge personality. "He is a salesman. Does he remind you of Avery?"

"He does. I reckon an airplane salesman's no different from a car salesman. Just makes more money."

Chapter Eight

Paul's meeting with his customer didn't go as he planned. After the customer learned the price of the airplane and the salary, he would have to pay a pilot he decided to fly commercial. His company still in the start-up stage couldn't take the expense. He spent the night at a hotel close to the airport before flying to Wichita to meet with his boss. This time, he checked the weather calling the airport twice before he left his hotel for the trip home.

His flight was uneventful, but he kept a watchful eye out for another summer thunderstorm. The meeting with Mr. Reynolds went better than he expected. The ornery man was in a good mood. He advised him to contact the customer every month in case he changed his mind.

After the meeting, he went to the Cessna Aircraft Company to see his friend, John Parks. John worked as an engineer and designer of airplanes. All through college they planned their future. They'd work side by side to design the new ships. His father had other plans. Matthew Williams got his son a job at Beech Aircraft Company. When Matthew told him about the job, he believed he had a position as an engineer, never dreamed he would fly airplanes around the country as an airplane salesman. "Good training for your job at Trans World Airlines," his father told him.

The taxicab pulled into the large parking lot and stopped at the main entrance of the building. He paid the driver and went inside the Cessna office. "Morning Mrs. Greene, I'm here to see John Parks. Is he in today?"

The phone rang, and the receptionist put the receiver to her ear with her hand over the mouthpiece. "He's in his office, go on back."

He stood in the door of John's office, stared at the drafting table and diagrams on the blackboard. This is what he craved, with a heavy heart he walked into the room.

His best friend glanced from his work and stood. "Hey, you're the last person I expected to see today."

"I had a meeting with Mr. Reynolds and decided to stop by."

John sat at his desk. "Have a seat."

"Thanks." He sat in the chair in front of the desk.

"How long are you staying?" He opened the top drawer, grabbed a piece of hard candy and pitched the treat to his friend.

Paul caught it and peeled the paper off. "Thanks. Just staying the night. I've got to get back to Georgia."

"How's the South?" The engineer leaned back in his chair and put his feet on the edge of his desk.

"Fine. The people are nice. I have my office at a small airport." He popped the candy in his mouth.

"Do they do much business?"

"Yes, they have more work than the three of them can handle."

John stared out his window then turned his head toward Paul. "That surprises me. I can't imagine a little hick town in Georgia with a successful airplane business."

"A lot of the big companies have private planes which need servicing. The ones who don't have airplanes hire Victor, Frankie or Lisbeth to fly them."

John raised an eyebrow. "Lisbeth?"

He brushed lint off his pants. "Victor's sister. He owns the airport. Frankie Howard, you may remember him. He was a famous barnstormer."

"Tell me more about the girl. I can tell by the way you say her name, she's special."

He gazed out the window, sucked on the candy in his mouth and pictured Lisbeth's face. "She's the most beautiful woman I've ever seen. She has eyes the color of sapphires and long dark hair."

"She's a pilot?"

"Yes, hell of a pilot, and a mechanic. Her brother said she knew more about engines than him or Frankie. She had an engineering book on her desk. Same one we studied in college."

"Damn, man, you're in trouble. Never seen you this excited about a girl. How far have you gotten?"

"Taking her to dinner Friday night."

"Didn't think you would take to a southern girl."

He gazed around the room and imagined himself working here. "Yes, it was quite unexpected."

John handed him a flyer. "You seen this?"

He read the announcement.

Chambers Trophy Air Race
Miami, Florida to Cleveland, Ohio
Prize: Trophy and $5,000
Date: Saturday, August 26, 1939

"Five thousand dollars is a lot of money." He imagined flying the race with Lisbeth.

"If I flew as your navigator, we could split the money. Twenty-five hundred is a lot of dough."

Paul folded the paper and put it in his pocket. "I need to think about it."

"What's there to think about unless you'd rather enter the contest with your fly girl."

He stood and walked to the door. "We'll see. You want to come by the house for dinner tonight?"

His best friend moved to the drafting table. "It's been a long time since I had some of Miss Lillian's cooking. Is dinner still at seven?"

"It is. I'll let her know you're coming."

"Is your father in town?"

He scratched the back of his neck and rolled his head around trying to release the tension that gathered anytime his father's name was mentioned. "I don't know. I guess we'll find out tonight."

The taxicab made its way down the long driveway toward the family estate. His mother inherited it when her parents died along with a good deal of money. Before she died, she contacted a lawyer and left her entire estate and all of her money to him with a request he keep Mr. And Mrs. Harper on until they retired or left for other jobs. To outsiders, Marjorie Williams lived a privileged existence but in reality, she endured a philandering husband who gambled their money away.

Matthew Williams was furious and sought the help of a lawyer to fight the will. The judge ruled Marjorie was in her right mind when she wrote it. He lost control of the house and money, so he turned to controlling his son.

The house sat back in the trees off the road. During the summer you couldn't see the home until you turned the last corner. He paid the driver and climbed from the backseat holding his suitcase.

Mr. Harper rested his hedge clipper on the ground and walked toward him. "Paul, good to see you. Need any help?"

He put his bag down and gave Wilfred a hug. "No, just one suitcase today. How are things here?"

"Quiet, Mr. Williams has been out of town, but we expect him this afternoon."

He hoped he could avoid his father, but he'd show respect. "It's good to be home even if for one night. Glad to see everything is fine here."

Lillian opened the front door and hurried down the steps. "Paul, welcome home. We've missed you."

He hugged Mrs. Harper. "I've missed home. I hope you don't mind, I've invited John for dinner."

Lillian put her hands on each side of his face and squeezed. "Just like old times with you two boys in the house. It's too quiet around here since your mother died. Your father spends more time in the air than he does in his home."

He knew where his father spent his time but didn't comment. He entered the foyer, various colors of roses spilled from a large vase on the round table. The ticking of the Grandfather Clock welcomed him.

He closed his eyes and breathed in the scent of lemon oil and moth balls. He pictured his mother running down the stairs to meet him. He climbed to the second floor, stopped by her bedroom, opened the door and peeked in. Her comb and brush set sat on her dressing table along with a perfume bottle and lamp. The room still smelled of her Chanel Number Five perfume. He closed the door and hurried to his room eager to put space between him and his memories.

****

Paul and John sat in the library enjoying a before dinner whiskey when Matthew arrived. He sat his drink down and poured the amber liquid in his father's favorite glass.

Matthew sipped the liquor. "This is quite the surprise." He nodded to John. "Good to see you."

He swallowed his whiskey in one gulp. "How've you been, father?"

"Busy, and you?"

"Malcolm's keeping me busy flying around the South selling airplanes." He poured another finger of Calvert into his glass.

His father addressed John. "How's the airplane design business at Cessna?"

"Never better. We're coming up with some interesting ideas, but I can't tell you with a Beech man listening."

He crossed his hands over his chest. "You calling me a spy?"

"Just kidding, but I still can't tell." John sipped his whiskey.

Miss Lillian stood in the doorway. "Gentlemen, dinner is served."

The men made their way toward the dining room.

The housekeeper set the table with china and flowers like Marjorie requested when she was alive. "Food's on the side board. Help yourselves. Let me know if you need anything."

Matthew stepped to the buffet. "Thanks, Lillian. This looks good."

Paul motioned for his guest to go ahead of him.

"Have either of you had fried okra? I had some at a bus stop restaurant in Saplingville. It was delicious."

Matthew arranged his plate on the table and sat down. "I had okra in gumbo in New Orleans but never had it fried. How do you like Georgia?"

He scooped mashed potatoes on the plate with his lamb chop. "It's hot and humid but the people are nice."

"TWA's hiring." Matthew's eyes met his sons.

He sat his plate on the table. "I'd rather sweat."

His father settled in his chair at the head of the table. "We'll discuss this later."

John savored a bite of lamb. "Wow, this is delicious. I've missed Miss Lillian's cooking. I was telling Paul about the Chambers Trophy Air Race. I think we'd have a good time and if we win, the prize is five thousand dollars."

Matthew's gaze flickered between the two men. "Winning the contest would prove good for your resume and get you ahead of other pilots in the job market. John, I assume you'll perform the navigator duties?"

"That was my plan unless Paul decides he wants to fly with his lady flyer."

Matthew put his fork down. "What the hell is a lady flyer?"

Paul glared at his friend bidding him to shut up. "There's a woman working at the small airport in Georgia who flies."

Matthew went back to eating his dinner. "Well, she sure as hell isn't anything compared to Amelia Earhart or Louise Thaden."

He mouthed to his friend, "Shut up."

John gave him a mischievous smile and ate in

silence.

He wouldn't let his father make fun of her. "Lisbeth Rose Douglas could give both of those women a run for their money."

His friend stifled a laugh with a drink of water.

Matthew smirked. "Sounds like you're thinking with the wrong head. Careful, don't ruin your life with a southern tart."

He would not let him push his buttons. "Careful is my middle name."

Chapter Nine

Lisbeth applied face powder and rouge to her cheeks. She wet a small brush with water and ran it through the black mascara cake and applied the black cream to her eyelashes. Paul would fly in today and she wanted to look presentable plus she had to shake the depression from her confrontation with the irate customer. She hadn't told anyone about their plans and dreaded telling her mother. Her ma would be happy if they eloped on the first date.

"Breakfast is ready. You're going to be late for work." Hattie called from the bottom of the stairs.

"Coming." She pinned her hair on her head and pulled on her cap.

A bowl of oatmeal flavored with butter and sugar along with a cup of hot tea sat on the table waiting for her. Hattie squeezed her daughter's chin with her thumb and forefinger. "Make-up? Since when did you start wearing make-up to work?"

She jerked her head away. Her cap came off and her hair escaped the pins. "I felt like it, okay?" She spooned a bite of oatmeal into her mouth and washed it down with the tea.

Hattie sat at the table across from her. "Is Paul coming into town today?"

She faced her mother and waited for the third degree. "Yes, and don't expect me for supper tonight."

"You have a date?"

"Yes."

"With Paul?"

"Yes, Ma."

"Well, Hallelujah." Hattie rung her hands in excitement.

She took another bite of oatmeal and had trouble swallowing. "It's a date, Ma, nothing more."

"Well, you haven't had one in so long I figured you'd planned to join a nunnery."

She put her spoon down. "I can't eat anymore; I'm not hungry this morning."

Her mother gave her a brown paper bag filled with her lunch. "Suit yourself. Here, take an apple in case you need a snack this morning."

She put the apple in the bag and grabbed her car keys. "See you tonight, Ma."

She spent the morning with Frankie working on the old bi-plane. The Curtiss JN-Four needed tender loving care. They replaced the spark plugs and greased the valve gears.

Frankie inspected the fuel line. "Fuel line is fine, no cracks or splits."

She squeezed his arm. "You are obsessed with fuel lines. Get over it. I know you checked the Jenny over before you flew with Ruth Ann. The emergency landing with her couldn't be helped."

He ran his hand over the black tube. "I know, but the incident scared the hell out of both of us."

"I think it was what my sister needed to come to her senses and admit she loved you."

He grinned. "Yeah, that too. You wanna fly her to her new home?"

She climbed on the wing and jumped in the seat. "Sure do, prop me off."

He headed toward the front of the plane. "I'll meet you at the new hangar."

Lisbeth guided the airplane into the air. She loved the old plane almost as much as Frankie and Victor. Al built a new shed for the Jenny for Frankie's birthday present. He constructed it on the right side of the main hangar so everyone would see the antique plane when they pulled into the parking lot of Andrews Field.

She landed, and the men pushed the bi-plane into the shed.

Al chocked the wheels. "Congratulations on a perfect loop the loop."

She helped with the tie down. "Never can resist that trick, it's my favorite."

Frankie gave Al a hug. "Thanks for building this for us."

The old man hugged back. "Never liked the idea of the Jenny out of sight in the open field."

The twin engine approached the airport. Her stomach turned over more than when she did the aerobatic trick in the Jenny. She put her hand over her eyes to block the sun. "Paul's here."

Al observed her and grinned. She caught his glance and rolled her eyes. "What?"

He pointed to the approaching plane. "It's Friday. He said he would see us Friday and…"

She put her hands on her hips. "And what?"

Frankie approached. "Someone care to fill me in?"

The handy man stepped back so she couldn't hit him and in a sing song voice said, "Lisbeth has a date."

Frankie stared at her. "You and Paul?"

She glared at them both. "Yes, he's taking me to Randall's."

Victor joined them. "Y'all are having too much fun."

She chased the men. Her hat came off her head.

Her brother picked it up as the Twin Beech came in for a landing. "The airplane salesman's here."

Frankie stood behind his boss. "Lisbeth and Paul have a date tonight."

Victor grabbed his sister and pulled her hands behind her back. "Why is this the first we've heard?"

She broke free and smoothed her hair. "Cool it. Let's act like we have manners. Here he comes."

Paul strolled to the foursome. "From the air, the activity in the parking lot looked like a grammar school at recess."

She stuffed her hair under her cap. "The boys had a little fun at my expense, nothing new."

Victor shook his hand. "Did you have a good week?"

He followed the others to the hangar. "Didn't sell anything. I flew to Wichita for a meeting and picked up more clothes from home."

Victor stopped inside the door. "Where to next week?"

He let his eyes adjust to the darkened hangar. "Birmingham, Alabama."

The boss headed toward his office. "Oh, by the way, any trouble in the storm Monday?"

He put his brief case on his desk and turned on his lamp. "Yeah, I got right in the middle of it. Next time I'll listen to you."

Frankie searched the tool box for a screw driver.

"You guys are wimps, that's when flying gets interesting."

He shook his head. "Not everyone has a dare devil spirit."

Lisbeth changed into a pair of slacks and a sleeveless top and left her coveralls hanging on a wall peg. She ambled by his desk on her way out the door.

Paul talked on the phone but raised his index finger and motioned for her to sit in a chair beside his desk. He ended the call and placed the receiver on the cradle. "Are you leaving?"

"No, I have a lesson this afternoon." Her heart beat faster, and she feared he would see the thumping through her blouse.

He lowered his voice. "I'll pick you up at six thirty, if that's all right."

Her student entered the hanger. "Sure, works for me. See you then." She stopped at her desk for her notebook and pen ready for the hour flying lesson.

After the successful session they secured the airplane and made an appointment for the following week. She walked to the hangar to file the paper work.

Al walked toward the door with a bag of trash for the burning barrel. "You 'bout ready to go Missy?"

She headed to her desk. "I need to take care of some business. You can go, I'll lock up."

"You have a fun time tonight."

"Thanks, Al. Tell Ethel hello for me."

"Will do. See ya Monday bright and early."

She opened her desk drawer and pulled out the June issue of Popular Flying. She found the ear marked page and read the job listing. Paul lived in Wichita and worked for Beech Aircraft Company, but he must know someone at Cessna who could help her get an interview. She weighed the pros and cons of telling him. She glanced at her watch. Five o'clock. She grabbed her clutch bag and keys. She couldn't leave him waiting or her mother would give him the third degree and he'd never ask her out again.

Chapter Ten

Paul raised his hand to knock on the screen door. The door opened, and he jerked his hand back.

Hattie Douglas stood in the door smiling at him. "Do come in." She raised her voice and addressed her husband. "Jacob, come say hello to Paul."

Mr. Douglas walked from the parlor and shook hands with him. "Good to see you. Come in and have a seat."

He walked toward the parlor when a beautiful site caught his eye. His date descended the stairs in a red dress cut low enough to see the mounding of her beautiful breasts, while the tight waist accented her curves. A pearl hair pin secured the dark hair on her head. A rose beaded purse in red velvet hung on her arm. He reminded himself to breathe. "Lisbeth Rose, you are beautiful."

Hattie laughed. "Oh, we call her Lisbeth. Plain ol' Lisbeth. We called her Lizzy until she turned thirteen and demanded we call her by her given name."

He faced her mother. "Mrs. Douglas, there is nothing plain about your daughter."

She put her hand over her heart. "Why, Paul, I believe you're right."

She kissed her father's cheek and hugged her ma. "I'm ready to go."

He opened the car door for the stunning beauty, her

scent floated through the air. She smelled like fresh cut roses. Hattie stood on the porch watching. He waved and smiled. "I'll have her back early, Mrs. Douglas."

Her mother waved. "See that you do."

He guided the car toward Main Street. His knees shook, and it was hard to navigate the clutch and gears. No woman had ever made him nervous, but he'd never met anyone like her. "I need you to direct me to the restaurant. I haven't journeyed out of Saplingville."

She placed her pocket book on the seat beside her. "It's easy. Drive to Main Street and head out of town. The restaurant's on the same road."

They made small talk and he relaxed and enjoyed the drive. He guided the car into Randall's Steak House parking lot. "I hope the food is as good as it smells." He turned off the ignition.

She reached for the door handle. "This is the best restaurant in the county."

He grabbed her arm. "Wait, I'll come around and open the door for you."

The restaurant was full with people standing in line for a table. Lisbeth squeezed her way through the throng of folks to the host. "I called earlier for reservations for two for Paul Williams."

"Yes, right this way."

He followed her. "Thanks, I had no idea it would be this crowded."

She turned her head toward him. "It's always packed on the weekends."

He held the menu and glanced at his date. He watched her as she studied the menu. She was breathtaking, the eyes of every man in the room followed as they walked to their table. If they were in

Wichita, he would take her home and… He looked into her blue eyes and wondered what she tasted like. She stared back. He found his voice. "What are you having?" He shook off the trance she had him under.

She held his gaze. "My favorite is filet mignon with boiled potatoes and tossed salad."

"I'll have the same. Do they have wine?" He put his menu on the table.

"Not in this county." She drank a sip of water.

"Too bad. A good red would go perfect." He gave the waiter their order and handed him the menus.

She folded her hands in her lap. "How was your week?"

"Good. I flew to Wichita for a meeting and spent time with an old friend and my father."

"Does this old friend have a name?" Her right eyebrow raised a millimeter.

He stared at her and grinned. "John Parks."

"Is he a pilot?"

"He has his pilot's license. He's an engineer and designer for Cessna, we've been friends since grade school. We both graduated from the University of Kansas, School of Engineering."

"You have an engineering degree." She sat straighter in her chair.

"Yes, all through college we talked of designing new ships together."

"But you decided to fly instead?"

He gazed around the restaurant and lowered his voice. "Yes, now I'm flying instead. Enough about me. How was your week?"

"I riled a customer."

"What happened?" He smeared butter on a cracker.

"Frankie flew a business man to Savannah, and I finished the engine repair he was working on. The customer found out and threw a fit. Victor told him to find someone else to work on his airplane from now on."

"I'm sorry." He reached for her hand and cradled it in his.

"It's okay, he's a jerk. Nothing any of us did pleased him."

"Well, sounds like you don't need his business anyway." He released her hand as the waiter placed glasses filled with iced tea on the table.

"Victor told me I would have a problem with arrogant men if I continued toward my path in a man's world." She squeezed a lemon wedge in her glass.

His father harbored prejudice against women and southerners. The bigotry passed down from the Williams men before them. Matthew Williams respected famous women flyers but had nothing but harsh words to say about ordinary women who tried to break into the field. He remembered what he himself had said about Lisbeth, he was his father's son even with his desire to become a kinder man than his father. "Well, after you get married and have children you'll forget about these encounters." He realized he'd said the wrong thing when fire flew from her blue eyes.

She drank a swig of tea and sat the glass on the table. She lowered her voice to almost a whisper. "Why do people think because I'm a woman I have to get married and have kids?"

He had to soothe her before he ruined their date. "Calm down, tiger. I'm sorry, I didn't mean to offend you."

She gave him a slight smile as the waiter positioned their salad plates on the table. She raised her tea glass to make a toast. "I'll be nice, if you will."

He clinked her glass with his. "Deal."

The waiter brought their steak and potatoes. He cut into the meat. "This is cooked perfectly. How's yours?"

She wiped her mouth with the white cloth napkin. "Delicious."

He stared at his beautiful date, *no Lisbeth Rose, you're the delicious dish.* He'd almost said it out loud. She had no idea every man in the room noticed her. "This is a nice restaurant reminds me of some steak houses back home."

"Yes, it's one of the best restaurants in the area. The pecan pie is as good as Ma's."

He wiped his mouth with his linen napkin and placed the cloth in his lap. "I bet you didn't tell your mother the pie tasted like hers."

"Oh, no. Ma thinks she's the best cook in the county and I refuse to tell her she isn't."

He paid the bill and placed his hand on her back as they walked out of the restaurant to signal the other men that she was taken. After settling her in the car, he sat in his seat, put the key in the ignition and pushed in the clutch ready for the trip back.

She scooted over in the seat and kissed him on the cheek. "Thanks for the lovely dinner."

He released the clutch, pulled her in his arms and gave her a gentle kiss on her lips. "You're welcome. Thanks for going out with me. Is there somewhere we can park and talk? It's too early to take you home."

She settled in her seat. "I know the perfect place."

He followed her directions. "Seems we're headed

toward Andrews Field."

"We are. Drive past the airport and turn right at the next gravel road."

He stared at the lake he flew over each time he landed at the airfield, stopped the car, and turned off the ignition. "Your uncle's lake?"

"Yes, there's a bench where we can sit and talk."

He opened her door and put his arm around her waist drawing her close. Twilight gave enough light for him to see the bench close to the water. He waited for her to sit and then he sat, held her hand and placed a kiss on her cheek. He stared at the sky as the stars came out one by one. "This is a magical place."

She placed her hand on the back of his neck and pulled his face close.

He gazed into her eyes. The jolt of his gut reaction unnerved him. She'd been sealed in his heart since the day he met her and if he kissed her the way his lips wanted there would be no going back. Her mouth enticed him, soft and willing. Instead of kissing her lips, he placed a chaste kiss on the top of her head. She put her arms around his neck, her body melted into his. Every woman before her, every disappointment, every happiness sabotaged by her embrace. He brushed kisses on the velvet skin of her neck and obeyed his heart. He fell into her snare and captured her mouth, devouring the sweetness of her lips, her response as eager as his. He kissed her neck making his way to the smooth mounds peeking from her dress. Her sighs and whimpers along with the growing strain in his pants drove him over the edge. "Lisbeth Rose." He groaned. God, she was some kind of woman.

She pulled him close and kissed him, slipping her

tongue in his mouth.

This was a woman who wasn't afraid to take what she wanted, and he liked it. He looked forward to taking her to bed, but he wouldn't ravage her outside with mosquitoes lurking around. He'd plan the elegant and beautiful adventure she deserved.

He stood and pulled her close. "I've got to get you home, Angel."

She placed a sweet kiss on his mouth. "Thanks for dinner. I had a wonderful time."

The soft huskiness of her voice radiated through him. He devoured her mouth one more time and memorized the shape of her lips and the feel of her body against his. "Let's go." He took her hand and led her to the car.

He opened her door. "Want to go to the picture show Sunday?"

She adjusted the hem of her dress. "If you'll have lunch with my family at Uncle Walter's house first."

He closed the car door and stuck his head in the open window. "Of course, I will, I'm addicted to southern food." He walked around the car. *I'm addicted to you more.*

He escorted her to the front door and started to kiss her when he noticed Mrs. Douglas staring out the window. "Does your mother always watch from the window?"

She pulled his face toward hers and kissed him on the lips. "Yes."

A grin spread over his face and he noticed the curtain swing and the front door open.

Mrs. Douglas pushed the screen door, they had to move fast to keep from getting hit. "Time to come inside Lisbeth." Hattie stood with her hands folded across her chest.

She ignored her ma. "See you Sunday."

He acknowledged her mother. "Mrs. Douglas."

Hattie closed the screen door but stood inside and watched.

He turned to go and stopped. "I'll pick you up at the Baptist Church. I want to check out the Methodist service this week."

She nodded. "Fine, see you then."

Paul made his way toward his car and chuckled. The more he learned about Lisbeth Rose Douglas the more he realized what a rebel she was.

Chapter Eleven

Paul worked in his room on Saturday and planned his strategy for the upcoming week. If he didn't sell more airplanes, he'd lose his job. Malcolm wasn't happy with his performance thus far. The salesman part with dinners, luncheons, and meetings were his forte and he liked the bull shit he dished out to the customers, but he didn't enjoy the flying. He studied a map to Birmingham, Alabama when Ella knocked on his door.

"Mr. Williams, you have a phone call."

He put the map down and raised his suspenders before opening the door. "Thanks, Ella." He followed her to the parlor with a sinking feeling in his stomach. He prayed his father's plane hadn't crashed.

He took the receiver and nodded to Ella as she went to the kitchen. "Paul Williams."

The female voice on the other end said, "Is this the Paul Williams who used to meet me in my barn at midnight?"

"Kathleen? Is that you sweetheart?" *How the hell did she get this number?*

"Yes, and I miss you. You came to town last week and didn't even visit. I'm very disappointed."

He recognized the sound in her voice, the one she used to get what she wanted. "It was a quick trip and I know you are busy with your debutante activities."

She sighed. "You know that was two years ago,

you and I had a big celebration for my entrance into society. Remember how much fun we had?"

He hadn't forgotten, it was the first time they had sex. "You're a volunteer for the program is what I meant."

Kathleen's voice changed. "Yes, I volunteer. I have to do something around here or I get bored. Speaking of bored, when are you coming home again? I miss you."

"Mr. Reynolds is keeping me busy selling airplanes. How'd you know where I'm staying?"

Kathleen giggled. "Are you trying to hide from little old me?"

"No." Yes, he wanted to say.

"John told me."

Kathleen could needle anything out of John. "You two are hanging out together?"

She purred. "Girls need attention and I don't get any from you."

"I'll see you next time I'm in town."

"Promise?"

He paused for a long moment. "Promise. Bye now."

"Good-bye."

He placed the phone on the cradle and scratched his head. His father pushed him to marry Kathleen because her dad was the richest oil man in town. But, to him, she was a spoiled brat and a good piece of ass.

****

Paul settled into his seat at the Saplingville First United Methodist Church. The organist played his favorite, 'Jesu, Joy of Man's Desiring' by J. S. Bach. The sound of the flute from the exposed pipes filled his ears. He closed his eyes and hummed. His mother played the tune on the piano and the music drew him to the afternoons he sat on the bench with her when he was a child. He loved watching her fingers glide over the keys. When he grew taller, he'd stand and watch the hammers hit the strings as she played the huge grand piano. God, he missed his mother.

The Methodist Church service inspired him, he left the sanctuary knowing he'd found a church home for his time in Saplingville. He drove to the New Hope Baptist Church and waited in the parking lot for Lisbeth. She exited the side door and walked toward his automobile.

He hopped out and opened the car door for her. "How was church?"

"Too long." She settled in her seat.

He walked around the car with a grin on his face. *She'll convert to Methodist or Presbyterian.* He started the car and backed out of the parking space. "Straight to your uncle's house?"

"Yes. The entire family's coming. I can't wait to see my niece and nephews." She gazed in her gold compact mirror and applied lipstick.

"Sweet kids." He changed gears as they sped down the main highway toward the airfield.

She snapped her purse closed. "Jake is a handful. He's named after my father and Al but he's as wild as Ruth Ann and Frankie when they were young. Ma says everyone has a child that pays them back for the grief they gave their parents." She patted her face with her handkerchief. "It's hot as hell today."

A smile spread across his face. He loved the way she changed from a gorgeous southern belle one minute to a tough broad the next. She didn't pout or whine like

Kathleen. Until he met her, he considered marrying Kathleen but now…well, now he had a bearcat to tame and he cherished the opportunity.

He visited with the men while Lisbeth played hide and seek with the kids. The other women helped in the kitchen.

Al cornered him. "So, you and Missy, huh?"

He stared at him. "Missy?"

Al nodded toward his date as she chased Jake into the room. "That's what I call her."

Lisbeth crawled around on the floor with the little tyke; he couldn't take his eyes off her. "We had a date Friday and she asked me to dinner today's all."

Al patted him on the back. "Yep, that's how it starts. Mind if I give you a little advice?"

"No." Paul listened.

Al pulled him aside, so no one could hear. "She's the sweetest girl I ever met until she's riled. Don't cross her. She's sweet as honey but tougher than any man I've known. She didn't get to where she is by fading into the background. She grabs life by the horns and hangs on."

He put his hand on the old man's shoulder. "You know, I think that's what I like most about her."

Jake ran to Al and he picked him up. "Well, just so you know."

He stood at the huge farm table; everyone joined hands while Walter prayed. He opened one eye and surveyed the family. Even Jake closed his eyes and folded his little hands under his chin.

As soon as Walter said 'Amen,' Jake reached for a biscuit. "Bikit, bikit, peez."

Delores broke a biscuit in half. "Here you go, little

man. Everyone, please sit and we'll start passing around the food."

The first dish presented to him was a platter of lettuce topped with pear halves brimming with mayonnaise and grated cheese and a cherry on top. "What's this?"

Walter spooned field peas onto his plate. "Pear salad. Trust me you'll like it."

He'd never seen such a variety of food. Lillian was a great cook, but she served a meat and two vegetables and yeast rolls, always. "You women sure know how to cook."

Hattie passed a bowl of sweet potatoes to Jacob. "Tell us Paul, is your mother a good cook?"

He drank a sip of sweet tea. "My mother died three years ago."

She placed her hand over her heart. "Oh, dear, I'm so sorry."

He wiped his mouth with his napkin. "Thank you. She was a wonderful woman but no, she didn't cook. Miss Lillian and her husband Wilfred live in the Carriage House on our property. He keeps the grounds and does upkeep on the houses. Miss Lillian cooks and cleans the house. I believed she was a great cook until I came here." Lisbeth put her hand on his leg, and he held it for support.

Delores said, "I'm sorry about your mother."

He raised his head and spoke. "It's me and my father now. He's a pilot for Trans World Airlines. He's gone from home more than he is there." He didn't mention his father's long-time mistress.

Victor spooned peas on Jack Andrew's small plate. "So that's how you came to flying?"

He addressed the interested faces. "Sort of, I have an engineering degree from the University of Kansas. My father has friends at Beech Aircraft who offered me a job after graduation. So here I am flying around the country selling airplanes."

Frankie juggled Jake on his lap, the child reached for the tea glass. "When did you learn to fly?"

He tore open a biscuit and slathered the tender bread with butter. "I started lessons at sixteen. When I saw you at that flying circus in Wichita, I decided then and there I wanted to fly an airplane."

"Your father didn't influence you?" Frankie spooned mashed potatoes into Jake's mouth.

"No, I never flew with him. When we went on vacation, we flew commercial. He encouraged me and found the best teachers when he discovered I wanted to learn. After I soloed my father and I would rent a Beech or Cessna and fly around Wichita."

Jacob listened to the airplane talk and raised his glass. "Let's salute our pilots. I never dreamed my son, daughter and son-in-law would fly airplanes for a living, but they are. Here's to flying and praying for safety for all involved. That includes our new friend, Paul."

Everyone raised their tea glass and joined in unison. "Here, here."

Chapter Twelve

The cotton mill bell roused Lisbeth from a deep sleep. She snuggled under the sheet enjoying the breeze from the oscillating fan. The realization she'd see Paul this morning brought her out of her stupor. She scrambled out of bed, put on her housecoat and slippers and drifted to the bathroom to get ready for the day. Desperate to look good for Paul she applied powder and rouge, forgoing the mascara. After several tries, the French braid in her hair appeared perfect. She stepped into the blue summer light weight coveralls Delores made for her. No grease on this pair...yet.

She arrived at the hangar and spotted his car. Her heart pounded and an ache settled in her belly. She entered the hangar and acknowledged her co-workers before settling in at her desk to read over the to-do list. Her brother delegated their work each morning and his airport operation ran like clockwork. Victor's military training in the United States Army Air Corps prepared him for his role as the owner of Andrews Field where they did everything from crop dusting, air taxis, airplane repairs, maintenance, and flight instruction. She glanced around the hangar. Paul leaned back in his chair. He winked at her and she rewarded him with a sexy smile.

He stood and grabbed his jacket, folded it over his arm and walked toward her desk. "Morning gorgeous."

She dropped the paper on her desk and stood. "Morning. Where are you off to this week?" He stepped close, the scent of Dunhill for Men cologne, the lavender, cedar wood, and touch of leather filled her nostrils. He stood before her impeccably dressed while she floundered in her handmade coveralls. He ran his index finger over the hand she had braced on the desk. Her breath caught as the electricity traveled up her arm.

He picked up the to-do list and read. "I'm headed to Birmingham, Alabama for customer meetings." He placed the paper on her desk and leaned close so only she could hear. "Can I see you this weekend?"

She gave him a quiet response. "Yes."

He stepped away and walked toward the door. "See everyone Friday afternoon."

Victor stood in his office door. "Have a safe trip."

Frankie and Al chimed in. "Safe travels."

She repaired a customer's airplane while Frankie gave two flying lessons. Three o'clock arrived and she checked off the last item on her list. Frankie sat at his desk flipping through a flight magazine.

She sat in the chair next to her brother-in-law's desk. "Are you done for the day?"

He put the magazine in his top drawer. "Yep, how 'bout you?"

"I've done everything on my list. You wanna teach me the Cuban Eight maneuver?" She stood, knowing he wouldn't refuse.

He grabbed his hat and goggles. "Sure. Get the headsets so I can talk you through it."

She entered her brother's office. "We did everything on our to-do lists, if you don't need anything else, we're going to fly the Jenny."

Victor held up one finger and wrote down a number on his ledger. "That's fine, y'all be careful."

"Always." She gathered the head sets and stuffed her hat, goggles and white scarf under her arm.

The men readied the Jenny while she tied the scarf around her neck and stuffed her hair into the hat. She secured the goggles on her head and adjusted the head set to fit. No matter how many times she flew, the anticipation of flight brought a flutter to her stomach.

She climbed in the back while Frankie sat in the front. The pilot always sat in the back seat of the open cock pit. If only one person flew the plane, the weight balanced.

She yelled, "Contact."

Al responded. "Contact." He pulled down on the propeller twice before the engine fired, then stepped away.

She commanded the runway and lifted into the air, her white scarf floated in the wind. She turned the bi-plane toward the lake away from her aunt and uncle's house. Aunt Delores terrified of flying did not like the tricks they performed. She did a barrel roll and a loop before flying the plane straight waiting for instructions.

"Great maneuvers, ready for the Cuban Eight?"

"Ready." His commands filled her ears as she memorized the steps.

"Start a loop, come down on the back side, do a half-roll into another loop, half-roll on the back side before pulling out."

She spoke into her headset. "Got it." Her first attempt proved clumsy, awkward and the loops uneven.

"Tighten up." Frankie advised.

She mentally drew a straight line through the lake

to use as a guide. She practiced the maneuver several times allowing time to fly around and get ready for each. After ten tries she accomplished her goal and the last two attempts close to what Frankie could do.

"Perfect." He spoke into the head set. "Fly through town and we'll call it a day."

She landed the bi-plane in a perfect three-point landing Frankie taught her. They disembarked from the plane and Al helped them place the Jenny in her private hangar.

The old man placed chocks under each wheel. "Great job, Missy."

"You could see us from here?" She helped tie the tarp over the plane.

"Victor and I drove over to the lake. It's 'bout time for y'all to put on an air show."

She untied her scarf. "Yeah, sounds like fun. You in Frankie?"

He led the way into the hangar. "Hell yeah, I'm in. We'll run it by the boss."

Victor spotted the three and motioned for them to come to his office.

Frankie entered first. "We were just talking about you."

He motioned for the group to sit. "Oh, yeah? Hope it was good."

She pointed to Al. "He had an idea about an air show here at the airfield."

The boss smiled. "Great idea, I think the townspeople would love a show." He handed a piece of paper to Frankie. "Paul gave me this before he left."

She leaned forward in her chair and read along. Excitement flowed through her. "I've dreamed of flying in an air race since the Women's Air Derby of nineteen twenty-nine."

Al read along and settled into his seat with a big smile on his face. "Five thousand dollars prize money is a lot of bucks."

Lisbeth stared into space. *Twenty-five hundred dollars would fund my move to Wichita. If I won, they'd take me seriously like Amelia, Louise and the other famous lady flyers.* She addressed her brother-in-law. "Can I fly, and you navigate?"

He stared at his sister-in-law while a smile bloomed on his face. "I think it's a great idea."

Victor chimed in. "Perfect plan. Frankie's flown all over the country, he can navigate the skies better than anyone I know. It's not about the fastest airplane or the greatest pilot, although that's very important, but knowing the best routes and staying the course along with a good airplane and pilot wins the race. We've got the best airplane for the trip, the Beech Staggerwing."

She couldn't sit still; she paced the room like a coyote circling his prey. "You'd let us fly it in the race."

"Absolutely."

She gave Frankie an anxious stare. "What do you think?"

He stood. "Let's do it, partner."

She shook his outstretched hand. "Let's win it."

Al said. "This is a better idea than the air show. I know you'll win. Those others don't stand a chance with a Lady Flyer and a Barnstormer.

Lisbeth drove her Chevrolet Coupe a little too fast on the way home. The air race pumped excitement through her to the gas pedal of the car. She reminded herself to slow down. All she needed was a ticket. She spotted Deputy Adam Riley parked behind a bush a block ahead. She slowed even more and waved as she passed. He'd stopped her one time and she'd not let it happen again.

She skipped in the back door. "What's for supper?"

Hattie removed bowls from the cabinet. "Chili and oyster crackers. For dessert, I have Neapolitan Ice Cream I bought at the store today."

She washed her hands at the sink. "Sounds delicious. Want me to tell Pa it's ready?"

"Yes, I'll put the food on the table."

She waited until her mother placed the green bowls loaded with two scoops of ice cream at each place setting before she brought up the subject of the air race.

Her mother's first words were. "That's too dangerous, all those planes racing through the air, what if you run into each other?"

Her father cackled. "It doesn't work like that, Henrietta."

She laughed with her father. "Pa's right. The time of take-off in Miami is reported to headquarters in Cleveland, Ohio. Each airport the pilot lands at relays the time of arrival and departure to the officials. Planes may veer off course or get stuck behind a storm, so navigation and knowledge of weather conditions play a big role."

Jacob placed his hand on his wife's. "I think it's a splendid idea. Anything your mother and I can do?"

She loved her father more in that moment than she ever had. He had her back and he'd support her move to Kansas. "Not that I know of."

****

The next day the excitement of the air race permeated the atmosphere of the hangar. In the afternoon after they'd finished work, they cleared off a work table and pulled out a map of the United States. She pointed to Columbia, South Carolina. "That's half-way. Will we stop there?"

Frankie scribbled some numbers on a piece of paper and made some measurements with a ruler. "Maybe." He put another map on the table. This one showed railroads running through the eastern United States. "We can follow Seaboard Air Line Railroad tracks to Jacksonville, Florida and pick up Southern Railway tracks into Ohio."

She studied the railroad map. "Iron Compass?"

"Yep, that's how we barnstormers did it. Never got lost. I'll get us there, you fly the Staggerwing into the wind and we'll win this."

Al approached them. "Planning your strategy?"

She wrote down major cities with large airports on a sheet of paper. "Yes, this is so exciting. How many times do you think we'll have to stop?"

"Depends on how often you have to pee." Al chuckled.

She continued to make notes. "I don't think I'll drink water for a week before we go."

The handy man said, "Frankie can pee in a cup."

"Not in my plane." She gave the old man a stern look, then her face broke into a smile and her laughter filled the room. "Hell, I don't care if he pees out the window, just so we win."

Chapter Thirteen

Paul flew in from Birmingham, Alabama Friday morning anxious to see his girl. He had plans to fly her to Atlanta Saturday, take her to the Fox Theatre to see the movie, *Jesse James,* and spend the night at the Georgian Terrace. If he read her correctly, he believed she'd go. At least he hoped with all his heart she would. He grew tired of the prying eyes in Saplingville. He needed some alone time with her to gauge his growing desire and make sure she liked him as much as he liked her. And if she insisted on two rooms, so be it.

He arrived at Andrews Field and strolled into the hangar, the large door stood open with fans shifting hot air through the area. Lisbeth's car sat in the parking lot and he searched the office for her. "Afternoon, everyone."

The men stopped their activities and greeted him.

Victor shook his hand. "How'd it go in Alabama?"

He nodded to the others. "Sold a Staggerwing to a physician. He's got a small Cessna but wanted to get a larger plane. He ordered a yellow one."

Frankie acknowledged him. "I'd shake your hand but I'm too greasy. He's a lucky man; Staggerwing's the best ship out there right now. We love the red one. Customers love to fly in it, too. It's smooth and has power. Thanks for the information flyer, Lisbeth's over the moon excited. We already sent in our application."

A wave of jealousy stunned him. He wanted to fly the air race with her. He'd already made plans to fly with John so why did he feel disappointed? "Who's the pilot?"

"Lisbeth, of course, I'll navigate."

He responded. "Entering with my friend, John Parks. I'm the pilot on our team."

Al pushed his broom along the floor. "Tight competition with a famous Barnstormer and a Lady Flyer teaming up."

The old man loved Frankie and his Missy as he called her, he reminded him of Wilfred. "What are you flying?"

Frankie pointed toward the red airplane. "The Staggerwing D Seventeen, of course, and y'all?"

"Staggerwing D Seventeen, Beech Aircraft is lending us a yellow one."

Frankie shook his hand. "May the best man, or woman win."

He glanced toward the runway as the yellow Cessna touched the ground. "May the best person win." His girl exited the airplane. "Need to speak to Lisbeth. Excuse me."

He deposited his brief case on his desk and hurried out the door. He waited until she finished with her student and greeted her with a kiss on the cheek. "I missed you."

She placed her hand on his arm. "I…missed you."

He looked into her blue eyes, the same color as her coveralls. "New work suit?"

She wrote the date and time on her paper. "Yes, Aunt Delores makes them for me. How'd you know it was new?"

"No grease stains."

She walked toward the hangar. "I try to keep at least one pair clean, so I can wear them when I teach, easier than changing into street clothes."

He grabbed her hand. "Wait, I need to talk to you about something."

She faced him. "You've got my attention."

He glanced around to make sure no one listened. "I made some plans for the weekend and I hope you will agree to them."

Her eyebrow rose. "What kind of plans?"

His belly did a somersault and his pants tightened with the anticipation of spending the weekend alone with her. "I want us…I mean, I hoped you would agree to accompany me to Atlanta Saturday morning. I have tickets to the Fox Theatre Saturday night to see *Jesse James* and reservations for the night across the street at the Georgian Terrace Hotel." He waited for her to answer, not taking a single breath.

She gave him a slight grin and didn't speak for a moment. "I'd love to."

A deep breath entered his lungs. "I can get two rooms if…"

"Not necessary." She winked at him.

If the bulge in his pants didn't go down, he'd have to jump in his car and leave to make space between them. "I'll pick you up at ten in the morning. We'll fly, it's quicker." *Why did I say that? She'll think I'm desperate.*

"I would love a night in Atlanta…with you."

He would have flown her to the moon, if she asked.

They made their way into the building, the air around them crackling with anticipation of the weekend. He strolled to his desk, but he wanted to kick up his heels and shout. He glanced around; no one paid him any attention. He opened his brief case and found the paperwork from the sale and called his boss.

She sat at her desk and gave him a smile like a cat that ate the canary. She finished her paperwork and walked into the bathroom. Watching her walk by, his thoughts drifted to the upcoming weekend until his ears caught up with his boss' comments. He concentrated on his paperwork and conversed with Malcolm. The bathroom door opened. He glanced up to see her dressed in her greasy coveralls to continue the work on the airplane engine she'd been re-building. He finished his work and ended the call. He made several more calls to set up appointments for next week in Chattanooga, Tennessee. He would have all his work done before he went to the boarding house. No distractions this weekend, he would concentrate on one thing, Lisbeth Rose.

He turned off his desk lamp and grabbed his brief case. She didn't see him until he stood before her. She concentrated on the engine with a determination he'd never seen before. "I'm done for the day. Got to go to the post office and do a little shopping in town. I'll see you in the morning. I'll pick you up at ten o'clock."

She wiped sweat off her face with a clean rag. "Of course. Have a nice evening."

He hesitated. He'd missed her this week and wanted to stay and talk but she had work and he needed to get the signed papers in the mail. He also wanted to stop by the men's store in town and purchase something new to wear this weekend. "Bye, now."

She removed her hat and her hair fell around her

shoulders. "Until tomorrow morning."

He wanted to rake his hands through her soft hair and kiss her juicy lips. She had no idea how hot he was for her. He didn't feel his feet touch the ground as he glided to his car. He'd never been this crazy about a woman, but he'd never met anyone like her.

At Main Street Men's Wear, Mr. Billings assisted him with his purchase of a quadruple windowpane jacket in light gray, white flannel trousers, white buckskin shoes and a straw hat. He had a light gray shirt and the perfect tie in his room.

The seamstress measured his pants for the length. "I'll have the pants cuffed and the suit sleeves hemmed and ready in two hours."

He admired his new suit. "Perfect, I'll return after I run my errands. Thank you." After the post office he headed to Price's Jewelry Store. He browsed the glass cases until he found what he came for.

Mr. Price stepped to the counter. "You've got good taste, these are quite expensive necklaces. You new in town? Haven't had the pleasure of your acquaintance. Homer Price."

He shook the man's hand. "Paul Williams. Pleased to meet you. Saplingville is my temporary residence. I'm from Wichita, Kansas.

"Yes, you're the fellow that sells airplanes and lives at the boarding house."

He'd never get over how fast gossip spread through the little town. "That's me."

"What can I help you with today?"

He surveyed the fine jewelry. "Let me see the sapphire necklace."

Mr. Price unlocked the case. "Beautiful piece but

quite expensive."

He examined the square sapphire stone surrounded by diamonds. He turned the box over and checked the price. *She's worth every cent.* "I'll take it."

"Gift wrapped?" The jewelry store owner eyed him.

"Of course." He wouldn't tell who would receive the gift, if he did, she would know by the time he picked her up in the morning.

He stopped by Douglas Drugstore for a quick egg salad sandwich before heading to the boarding house. Between the heat of the night and the excitement of the coming day, he didn't drift to sleep until after midnight. As usual, he woke to a cool morning and snuggled under his sheet until the sun beamed through the curtain. He jumped out of bed and headed to the bathroom to shower and shave before the other boarders woke and he'd have to stand in line.

He dressed in his new suit and packed his suitcase. He put the gift in his pocket. *Can't forget this.*

The Saplingville Diner held a packed house. He hung his hat on the rack and made his way to the counter.

Sally put out a cup and saucer and poured coffee. "Mr. Williams, you look dapper today. Where you goin' all dressed up like that?"

He studied the menu. "Now, Sally, you ask too many questions. Can't a man dress up and come to your place of establishment for breakfast without the third degree?"

She placed a fork, knife and spoon on a napkin. "You come in here looking like the fine dandy of a man you are and expect me not to flirt with ya?"

Joe yelled. "Order up."

He grinned. "Your husband's calling you."

She returned the coffee pot to the burner. "Back to reality, but a girl can dream cain't she?"

He put the menu down. "I'll have the pancakes and sausage this morning."

She grabbed the two plates filled with food. "Hey, Joe, order for pancakes and sausage plate."

Joe peered through the window and waved. "Morning Paul."

"Morning." He drank the hot coffee. The acceptance from the townspeople pleased him. He'd adjusted quite well to the South and the people.

Chapter Fourteen

Lisbeth woke early and enjoyed a leisurely bath scented with rose water, washed her hair and put on her bath robe before descending the stairs for breakfast.

Her ma slathered butter on bread and popped the pan in the oven. "Ready in two minutes, set the table, will you?"

"Sure, Ma." She wasn't going to mention her weekend until after breakfast; Hattie would be a problem but nothing she couldn't handle.

The family sat down to scrambled eggs, grits, bacon, toast, fig preserves and coffee.

She placed her plate in the sink. "Delicious breakfast, Ma. Thank you." She rinsed her plate and filled the dish pan with soap and water. "I'll clean up the kitchen."

"I appreciate that." Hattie took off her apron and hung it on the wall hook.

Lisbeth peeked in the parlor where her mother read a magazine and her father perused the newspaper. She hurried to her bedroom and slipped into a wrap-around blue dress with a V-neck and large collar. She considered pinning her hair in a loose chignon at the back of her neck but decided to let her hair be as free as she felt. She combed her tresses and let the silky mass fall at her shoulders. Her stomach did a flip when she pulled her overnight bag from under the bed. She would spend the weekend with Paul, alone in Atlanta. She took her prettiest lace nightgown from her drawer and caressed the satin to her cheek. Tonight, Paul's hands would caress her skin through the soft fabric. Her hands shook in anticipation of spending the weekend with him and the dread of facing her mother.

She strolled into the parlor where her parents sat in their chairs reading.

Her mother studied her appearance. "You're wearing one of your pretty dresses, you and Paul going somewhere today?"

She grabbed a magazine and sat. "As a matter of fact, we are. We're going to Atlanta this morning."

Hattie put her paper down. "What time will you be back home? I'll have a nice supper for y'all."

She glanced at her father. "He's taking me to a movie at the Fox Theatre tonight. I won't come home until tomorrow."

Jacob kept his face buried in the business section.

Her mother stood and glared at her with her arms crossed in a familiar stance. "You are not spending the night with him."

"He has reservations for us at the Georgian Terrace across the street, separate rooms, of course," she lied.

"What if someone sees you going into the hotel? How will they know you have separate rooms? They'll think...well, they'll talk about you. John Brown! I don't like this at all. Jacob?"

He put his paper down and stared at her over his glasses. "Henrietta, leave the girl alone, she said they would stay in separate rooms. Our daughter is grown; didn't you learn anything from raising Ruth Ann? You can't control these girls when they have grown into women. Whatever raising you've done is done. Too late to change it now."

She couldn't meet her daddy's eyes; it would confirm the truth. But he loved her unconditionally and believed in her like no one else. "He's picking me up at ten this morning. I have to finish packing my things." She went to her room and read a book until she heard the crunch of the gravel in the driveway.

She grabbed her clutch and suitcase and hurried down the stairs. "He's here."

Her parents met him at the door.

Jacob shook his hand. "Paul, how are you today?"

"Fine, Mr. Douglas, and you?"

"We are all fine, enjoying this nice Saturday morning. You have fun and be very careful in Atlanta."

Mrs. Douglas bounced from one foot to the other. "I don't see why you have to spend the night. We have movie theaters in Saplingville."

"I won't let anything happen to your girl." He retrieved Lisbeth's suitcase.

Hattie crossed her arms. "I don't like this one bit and I expect you to stay in separate rooms at the hotel. Y'all hear me?"

Jacob put his arm around his wife and pulled her close. "They are a respectable couple, Henrietta, they'll do what's right."

She pulled away from him and stared at her daughter. "They'd better."

Lisbeth gave her father and mother a kiss on the cheek. "See you tomorrow."

He started the car, pushed in the clutch and placed the gear in reverse. "I wondered what you would tell your mother. If it's separate rooms, I'll have to call and get another, because I only have one reserved." He gave her a questioning grin.

She placed her hand on his leg. "Not necessary, I want to be with you."

He raised her hand to his lips and kissed it. "I want to be with you, too."

Her pulse quickened, and heat radiated from her core. Her first sexual experience happened a few months ago with Perry Collins. Perry was handsome, and she'd known him since grade school. They went to a movie and drove to a secluded spot in the country to park and kiss. One thing led to another and she'd wanted to explore a sexual experience for some time. She refused to marry to have relations with a man like most of her friends did so she'd kept a prophylactic in her purse since last year, in case an opportunity presented itself. She basically seduced him. It was quick and over in an instant. Her body screamed for something more. He'd worried her to death for another date even hung around at the hangar until she told him Victor didn't allow visitors during work hours.

"What are you thinking about?"

His question pulled her to the present. "Nothing, just enjoying the ride. You gonna let your co-pilot fly a little today?" He down shifted the car and turned in the drive way of Andrews Field. "I sure will, you'll love how the Twin Beech handles."

He opened the co-pilot door and placed their luggage behind the seat. "Let me help you in."

She put her hand in his and ascended to her place. A scan of the instruments while she adjusted her seat and fastened her seatbelt caused her pulse to quicken. This was her world; she grew fully alive each time she took to the air. "I love this airplane."

"It's one of the best around."

He positioned the checklist behind his seat. "Ready for take-off?"

"Ready."

****

He signed the register as Mr. and Mrs. Paul Williams. He winked at her and smiled.

The employee gave him the key. "Have a nice evening Mr. Williams."

She floated over the Italian-tiled floor, her arm through his, and studied the Italian-bronze chandeliers and white marble columns. *So, this is how the rich people live.* "This is the most beautiful hotel I've ever seen."

He paused to let her enter the elevator first. "The tenth floor, please, sir."

The bellman entered with their luggage.

Paul gave her a seductive smile. Her entire body tingled in anticipation of the night to come. She willed herself to calm down. First, there was dinner and a movie.

He handed the elevator operator a dollar bill. She stared in disbelief.

They entered the large suite. He directed the bellman. "You can place the suit cases in the bedroom, please."

He presented the man with two dollars. The man bowed and left the room. She walked to the window and peered at the scene below bustling with people. Automobiles and trolley cars lined Peachtree Street; the marquee at the Fox listed Jesse James as the featured movie.

He put his arms around her waist, his cheek touched hers.

She closed her eyes and melted into his embrace.

He turned her toward him and placed a wrapped box in her hand.

"Paul?" She gave him a slight grin. "What's this?"

"A little present for my girl. Open it."

"You didn't have to get me anything. You are spending way too much money. I can't believe the tips you've been giving out."

He kissed the top of her head. "Sweetheart, you are worth every penny. If you don't open it, we won't make our dinner reservation."

She tore open the paper and raised the lid on the box. "A sapphire pendant, oh my, it's...the most beautiful necklace I've ever seen."

He released the necklace from the case. "Turn around, I'll fasten the clasp." She did as he asked. "Let me see."

She pivoted toward him and placed her fingers on the stone. "How's it look?"

His gaze went from her eyes to the necklace. "A perfect match for your blue eyes." He crushed her to him in a lingering kiss.

She parted her lips and met his smoldering kiss with her own; her senses reeled as if short circuited.

He stopped kissing her and drew her close. "Oh, my sweet Lisbeth Rose."

Her body screamed, make love to me, now. His arousal evident against her. Making love to him would be nothing like her first time with Perry. Everything was different about him, every feeling she experienced, every craving, and every desire magical and new.

He opened his suitcase and hung up his clothes for the next day. "Do you need to freshen up before we head to Ye Olde Herren's Restaurant for dinner?"

"We're going there?"

"Nothing but the best for you, sweetheart."

She hurried to the restroom and brushed her teeth and freshened her make-up. She'd read the restaurant reviews in The Atlanta Constitution newspaper, Herren's was touted as the restaurant of the elite. She assumed they would eat dinner here in the hotel. This entire trip was a surprise from the invitation yesterday to the necklace and now dinner at a fancy place. She checked her face in the mirror and blotted her lips on a tissue. *I am one lucky girl.*

He paid the taxicab driver. "We'll need you again in an hour and a half to take us to the Fox Theatre." He handed the man a dollar.

The driver nodded his head. "I'll be here, thank you."

He helped her out of the car and spoke to the driver. "Thank you, sir."

The Maître D' seated them and presented them with menus. "Your waiter will be right with you."

Sterling silver flatware and china adorned the table. She stared at the array and remembered the Etiquette Book Aunt Delores had given her. She called to mind the chapter on table settings and relaxed when she remembered the order to use each item. She studied the menu. The prices, holy cow, she couldn't afford to eat here on her salary. She glanced at her date; he seemed relaxed as he made his choice. *Beech Aircraft must pay him a lot of money.* She would not take advantage of him or his money, so she'd let him order for them.

"Everything on the menu looks delicious. I'll have what you're having."

The waiter appeared at their table and poured water in their glasses. "Are you ready to order, sir?"

He closed his menu. "Yes, we'll have the Caviar Canape for our appetizer. Two Special Sea Grill Salads, with the Riesling Wine. For our entree two Top Sirloin steaks, medium, Lyonnaise Potatoes and Burgundy Wine."

The man collected their menus. "Of course, sir."

"I've never had caviar before." She spotted a matchbook in the ash tray. "Do you think I could have the matchbook for a souvenir?"

He handed her the book of matches. "You can have anything you want."

She turned the matchbook over and read the cover.

'Ye Olde Herren's Restaurant
Famous for Seafood
84 Luckie Street, Northwest
Atlanta, Georgia
Take any cab and say Ye Olde Herren's.'

"I've dreamed of eating here. It's more than I imagined."

The waiter appeared and poured a small amount of Riesling into Paul's glass.

He inhaled the bouquet of the wine and drank a sip. "That's fine."

The waiter filled their glasses.

He raised his. "To us."

She clinked her glass with his. "To us." The dry wine went down smooth. "Delicious."

"Yes, it is." He winked at her before taking another sip.

A waiter placed the appetizer plate between them and placed small white china plates with a gold rim at each place setting. "Enjoy."

He put a toasted brioche round topped with sour cream and caviar on her plate.

She bit into the crunchy bread and closed her eyes. The saltiness from the fish roe tasted wonderful with the crunchy bread and smooth cream.

He studied her. "You like?"

"I love." She placed a second piece on her plate.

The wine made a perfect match with the Hors d'oeuvre.

A waiter materialized and cleared their dishes. Another presented the salad plates.

Condensation dripped from the cold salad bowl filled with lettuce, tomato, artichoke, avocado, crab, shrimp and lobster meat. A small pitcher of Thousand Island dressing sat next to each plate. She poured some dressing on the salad. Her first bite consisted of lettuce, avocado and lobster. She closed her eyes and savored the taste. "Oh, my."

He sipped his wine. "I'm happy you're enjoying the dinner."

His fork sat beside the salad bowl. "You haven't even taken a bite."

"I'm having more fun watching you."

Her face heated. "I'm acting like a country idiot who's never been out of my county, but this food is extraordinary."

He picked up his fork and knife. "Pleasing you, making sure you enjoy the food, the accommodations, it's all that matters to me."

"Thank you." She drank a sip of wine and enjoyed

every bite of her salad.

When they'd eaten their steak and potatoes, the waiter appeared and offered dessert. She couldn't eat another bite of anything.

Paul asked. "Would you like dessert?"

With every breath, her belly strained against her dress. "Not for me, thank you."

"Bring us both a small glass of Sherry, the best you have." He waited for the waiter to clear the table. "I'm glad you agreed to come with me this weekend. I'm tired of sharing you with everyone in Saplingville."

"Thank you for asking me. It's been a magical weekend."

He winked at her. "Oh, sweetheart, you haven't seen anything yet."

Chapter Fifteen

Paul guided his date through the crowd and out the door of the Fox Theatre. "Did you enjoy the movie?"

"Yes, the movie was great, but the Islamic and Egyptian architecture never ceases to amaze me. Thanks for getting seats in the front so I could see the crystal stars on the ceiling."

They glided across the street with his arm along her back. "I'll take you to the Fox Theatres in St. Louis and Detroit, sometime."

"You've been to those?"

"I have, and I'll take you. You'll love them. They're as beautiful as this movie palace." He paused as the doorman opened the door for them. "After you, my dear."

He walked toward the elevator, confidence in his step. Tonight, he would have Lisbeth; he would find his pleasure and make sure she found hers. If he could wrap her in a cocoon of silk and keep her with him, he'd do it. But she wasn't a girl he could coddle, or control and he loved that about her.

He unlocked the door to their room and allowed her to enter. He closed the curtains, removed his jacket and loosened his tie. She didn't move toward him, so he went to her and pulled her close. "Nervous?"

"No, excited mostly." She looked him in the eyes. "I guess a little nervous."

He brushed her hair behind her ear. "Have you made love to a man before?"

She swallowed and pursed her lips. "I wouldn't call what we did making love, but I'm not a virgin, if that's what you're asking."

He hugged her and kissed the top of her head; her hair, soft as silk, smelled like lavender. He'd make sure she'd forget about her awkward first time. She deserved perfection, and he would damn sure give it.

"I didn't think I'd ever find anyone. I should have waited, but I wanted to know what sex was about, so I seduced one of my dates," she said in a whisper.

"Where were you?" He remembered his trysts with Kathleen in the barn and wondered where Lisbeth experienced her first time.

"In the back seat of his car on a country road."

"That was one lucky son of a bitch." His last words extinguished by the touch of her lips. Her return kiss drugged him with desire. He entered a world he'd never been in, lust, sure; possessing her body, naturally; his heart bursting with…something, an ache that proved losing this woman would be his undoing. "Lisbeth Rose." He whispered her name and kissed her neck. He released the clasp on her necklace and placed the jewelry on the table.

She unbuttoned his shirt and placed his cuff links next to her necklace.

He stripped down to his undershorts and socks, never taking his eyes from hers. He watched as she released the clasp and belt of her wraparound dress to display the silky lace slip and her beautiful mounds peeping from her brassiere. "Oh, sweetheart." He buried his lips between her breasts as he tugged her dress and threw it on the floor.

She cradled his head in her hands and sighed. "Paul."

He snapped open the clasp and her breasts burst from their hold. She stood before him in her briefs and stockings. He explored her body outlining her nipples with his fingers. "You like?"

She closed her eyes and released a breath. "Yes, I like very much."

He sat on the bed, pulled her close, and snuggled his head between the creamy flesh of her breasts and explored each nipple. He sucked and teased until she melted against him.

"Stop, I can't take it anymore, please. God, what's happening to me?"

He stood and captured her mouth and accepted her hungry kisses as she explored the depths of his mouth with her tongue. His body tingled as she raked her nails over his back, her need of him evident with each moan and sigh.

"Please, let's make love, now," she begged him.

"No," he whispered.

She stepped back. "Did I do something wrong?"

He sat her on the bed and rolled her stockings down each leg. "Angel, I'm going to make love to you, but we are going slow, not like in the back seat of a car parked on some country road." He pulled her briefs off, lifted her, and placed her on the bed.

She kissed him and whispered, "Take off your clothes, now."

He sat on the bed, removed his socks, stood and pulled his shorts off.

He snuggled against her in the bed and kissed her

mouth; the feel of her naked body against his created a want he'd never known.

His lips explored every inch of her smooth ivory skin, as his hands searched for pleasure points. Her body had found a release minutes ago and she moaned and writhed against the sheets. He'd please her many times tonight to replace the memory of her first time with a bumbling idiot.

Her body arched toward him and she pleaded, "How can you wait any longer?"

He pulled her close, ready to make love to his angel.

She opened her eyes. "Wait, do you have a rubber prophylactic?"

In his haste to make love, he didn't even think about protection. He could care less if she got pregnant; he would marry this woman, come hell or high water. Getting her to agree would prove another matter. "Yes, I have one in my pocket."

He found the packet, stared at her lying before him, and burned the picture into his brain. He'd never forget this night and prayed it would not be their last.

He lowered himself to the bed and pulled her close until their bodies melded together. Flesh against flesh, woman against man. Making love to her was sensual, sexy and seductive. He was born to love this woman, born to please her and protect her. She cried out his name and he lost his mind in the bliss that was Lisbeth Rose. Their bodies were moist from sweat and desire and the sheets tangled around them. He kissed the top of her head. "Sweetheart, that is how you make love to someone."

She snuggled her head against his chest. "Yes, I see

the difference."

Her breathing slowed, the light from the lamp illuminated her dark hair; she'd found sweet slumber. He left her for a moment and turned off the light. He pulled her close and she snuggled her leg over him. The sheets tangled over their bodies. Now he knew what one flesh meant.

****

Dappled light burst through the curtain; he lay on his side with her spooned against him. She turned to face him. "Good morning."

"Good morning, did you sleep well?" He pushed her hair away from her face.

She snuggled against his chest. "Best night's sleep I've ever had." She whispered in his ear, "I think you're ready for another round."

"You think so, huh?" He tickled her until she laughed and begged him to stop while she kicked and struggled to escape. Their laughter and teasing transitioned into passionate kisses and urgent lovemaking. "Lisbeth Rose. My angel." He kissed her and pulled her close. He didn't want to get out of bed, didn't want to take her home, and didn't want to leave on his trip tomorrow.

He lay on his back with his eyes closed. He raised a lid half way; she stared at him with her sweet smile. "You look so happy." He pulled her close and rested his chin on the top of her soft hair.

"I am very happy but also hungry. What's for breakfast?"

He nibbled on her neck. "You, sweetheart, you're what's for breakfast."

She giggled. "I need food. You've worn me to a

frazzle."

He hesitated, not wanting to let her go. "I'll call room service. You bathe, and we'll eat when you're done." His eyes followed her as she walked into the bathroom. *God, she's beautiful.* He gathered their clothes off the floor and straightened the room before he called for their breakfast.

She walked from the bathroom wrapped in a towel and rummaged through her suitcase. She pulled out a lace gown. "Guess I brought this for nothing."

He took the negligée and pulled the towel off her. He placed the gown over her head and stared. "There, you've worn it and you look delicious." He kissed her; the intimacy in their kisses reminded him of what they'd shared.

A knock at the door interrupted the moment. "Room service."

She ran in the bathroom and closed the door.

He grabbed some money and presented it to the waiter. "Thank you."

The man bowed. "Thank you very much, sir."

He lifted the lids from the plates. "You can come out now, your breakfast is served."

He poured coffee into their china cups. "My goal was to feed you breakfast in bed and watch you eat naked as a jay bird but seeing you in your gown sitting at the table with me is a fine vision of loveliness."

She added sugar to her coffee and stirred. "You are such a romantic. This has been the most wonderful trip I've ever been on. I feel like a queen."

His lips grazed hers. "Glad you've enjoyed it." If he told her he loved her, she'd bolt. She'd made it clear a husband and family were not her priorities. *Don't scare her.*

She buttered her bread. "Scrambled eggs, potatoes, sausage, biscuits and fruit, this looks heavenly."

He picked up a crock. "Don't forget the peach jam."

"You're spoiling me. I'll never be the same after this."

He placed a spoonful of jam on her plate. "I get more joy out of pleasing you." He turned her face to his and kissed her lips. He pulled away and stared.

She opened her eyes and smiled. "Thank you for everything."

"Thank you for agreeing to come with me."

Chapter Sixteen

Lisbeth drew on all the acting skills Ruth Ann taught her to hide the truth from her mother and so far, the farce worked. Paul left Monday morning, but he called the hangar and talked to her Wednesday. She didn't realize how much she missed him until she heard his voice over the wire.

She sat at her desk and pulled out her lunch bag. She drank a sip of the cold bottled soda when she noticed a white envelope with gold banding in her inbox. The blue ink and insignia showed Cessna, Wichita, Kansas as the sender. Her stomach flipped, and she let out a large burp. She glanced around, Al stared and smiled.

She put her hand over her mouth. "Excuse me."

The old man ate his ham sandwich while he read the newspaper. "You're excused."

She grabbed her letter opener and sliced the envelope open. She scanned the note. *Miss Lisbeth Douglas, Thank you for your interest...we will hire five people...Contact me for an interview...Sincerely, Edward Miller.*

She placed the letter on her heart, closed her eyes and prayed. *Thank you, Jesus.*

She jumped from her chair and raced around holding the letter in the air. "I have an interview with Cessna in Wichita."

Victor walked to her desk. She handed him the letter. He studied the missive. "I didn't know you applied. A test pilot? This is great."

"I couldn't tell you, because I was afraid you wouldn't want me to go."

He hugged her. "Of course I don't want you to leave us but there's a whole world out there beyond Saplingville. You are destined for greater things."

Frankie came into the hangar from outside. "What's going on?"

Al stood with his hands on his hips. "Missy's leaving us, going to be a test pilot for Cessna."

He grabbed her and swung her around. "I am so proud of you."

She regained her balance. "Wait, we don't know if I'll get it. You know I have a big strike against me. I'm a woman."

Victor leaned against her desk. "Yes, you are and since they wrote you, it's to your advantage. Appears they're ready to hire a female pilot."

She glanced at the letter. "They did say they're hiring five people; maybe I have a chance."

Al hugged her. "Of course, you do, Missy. We'll miss you around here."

She stared at the three most dear people in her life. They'd formed who she was as a woman, a mechanic, and a flyer. How could she leave them behind? A tear slid down her face.

Her brother hugged her close and chuckled. "Don't cry; we're happy for you. We'll all miss you, but you can't pass up this opportunity."

She dried her face with her sleeve. "I know, but y'all mean so much to me."

Frankie piped up. "Kansas isn't very far as the crow flies. We all have a means of fast transportation. We won't go long without seeing each other."

She laughed. "Tell that to Ma. She's going to kill me."

"I think we need to keep Ma in the dark as long as possible." Victor walked toward the soda machine.

She sat at her desk and nibbled at her lunch, not tasting anything; anticipation of the phone call had her stomach in knots. The men continued their work, so she picked up the phone and placed a call to Cessna.

She fixed her eyes on the name at the bottom of the letter.

A female voice answered. "Cessna Aircraft, how may I direct your call?"

She stuttered. "Ed…Edward Miller, please."

"Of course, please hold."

She wanted to hang up the phone, her hands shook, and she cleared her throat.

"Ed Miller, how can I help you?" The male voice boomed over the line.

She twisted the cord. "Um, yes, this is Lisbeth Douglas, uh…Lisbeth Douglas from Saplingville, Georgia." She closed her eyes and forced the words from her brain to her mouth. "I received a response from the inquiry I sent regarding the test pilot job?"

"Yes, Miss Douglas, how are you?"

She didn't expect the small talk. "I'm fine, sir. And you?"

"Never better." He paused.

"I'm calling to make an appointment with you for the interview?"

He shuffled some papers. "Ah, yes, I have your

credentials in front of me. How about next week? Say …Thursday."

She paused to check her calendar. "What time?"

"Three o'clock good for you?"

She exhaled. "Three o'clock is perfect. See you Thursday at three. Thank you."

"Thank you for your interest. Good-bye, Miss Douglas."

"Good-bye." She clung to the receiver, not wanting to place it on the cradle. She wiped sweat off her forehead with a handkerchief and grabbed a nickel from the top drawer. The heat of the day and the excitement from the conversation left her dizzy and thirsty. She placed the coin in the soda machine, raised the lid, and pulled out a bottle. The oscillating fan blew hot air around her while the cold caramel drink energized her. At the sound of the roar of the Twin Beech she guzzled the drink, deposited the empty bottle in the wooden crate, and raced outside to watch Paul land.

He turned off the engine and exited the plane. "I missed you, sweetheart." He brushed her lips with a gentle kiss.

He looked comfortable with his sleeves rolled up to his elbows, clean and cool.

"I missed you," she whispered.

He reached for her.

She backed away. "I'll get grease and sweat all over your nice clothes."

"I don't care, I'll buy new clothes." He grabbed her and placed a tantalizing kiss on her mouth.

She pulled him close and deepened the kiss, melting into the embrace. Her core pulsed with need. She loosed herself from him while she still could.

"Something incredible happened today. I have an interview with Cessna next week." She searched his face for a reaction.

"Doing what?" He asked and returned the stare.

"Test pilot." If he was happy for her, she couldn't read it on his face. "What do you think?"

He pulled her close and enveloped her in a protective embrace. "Happy for you but frightened that you'll be a test pilot. It's dangerous, you know that don't you?"

She relaxed in his arms. "Yes, but there is danger every time we fly, you know that."

"I do." He raised her chin with his thumb. "What day is the interview?"

"Thursday at three in the afternoon," she whispered.

He removed his brief case from the plane. "I have to go to Wichita next week. I'll fly you and take care of business with Beech while you do your interview, and we'll stay at my house. I want you to meet Lillian and Wilfred, they'll love you."

"And your father, will he be there?"

They walked toward the hangar. "Don't know, he might. Who's your interview with?"

"Edward Miller."

He let her enter ahead of him. "Want me to put in a good word for you?"

She turned to face him. "No, please don't. I have to do this on my own."

"I understand." He acknowledged Frankie and Al and went to his desk.

She continued her paperwork, but Paul's gaze burned through her, the expression on his face one of concern. This was her chance, and if she lost him or her mother never spoke to her again, so be it. To want something this desperately had to be right, didn't it? If she were a man everyone would be happy for her.

He stopped by her desk. "Let's see a movie tonight."

Her laughter rippled through the hangar.

"What's so funny?" He asked.

"I'd love to, but you'll never believe what's playing this weekend."

He stared at her. "I have no idea."

She grinned. "*Test Pilot* with Clark Gable and Myrna Loy."

"How many times have you seen this movie?"

She stood. "Too many to count. Have you seen it?"

"Yes." He held her hand. "The movie shows how dangerous the job is. Two people die in the movie, for God's sake."

"Clark Gable's character was reckless. I'm not." She removed her hand from his and sat in her chair refusing to be bullied. "I don't want this to cause a problem between us, but I'm doing it, with or without you."

"I'll pick you up at seven." He left the hangar in a huff.

Chapter Seventeen

Paul examined the JN-Four from propeller to tail, then checked out the cockpit with the few gauges, pedals, and stick, amazed at the simplicity of the biplane.

"Check the covering and tug at the wires to make sure they're taut." Lisbeth climbed on the front wheel and stuck her head in the engine.

He'd seen his share of air shows, but he'd never been in an airplane while the pilot performed aerobatics. "Wires are tight, and the covering appears fine. What else?"

"Check the tires." She closed the cover on the engine.

Her sense of knowledge and confidence calmed his apprehension. He peered at the underside of the plane. "Did you check the fuel line?"

She grabbed her white scarf and tied the fabric around her neck. "You heard the story?" She gave him the hat and goggles.

He tugged the cap on. "Frankie told me. If the engine dies, can you land like he did?"

"Of course, I can glide the plane down, if we're near a clearing." She pulled the goggles over her eyes. "Are you scared?"

He hesitated. "No." A quick and disturbing image of crashing into the earth crossed his mind.

"It's…well…I've never ridden in an open cockpit or participated in aerobatics."

She positioned the goggles on his head. "Do you get motion sickness or is it your fear of heights?"

"Fear of heights, I guess, although I feel stupid admitting my fear, although I think it's more common in pilots than you think." He offered his hand to help her into the plane.

She settled in her seat. "Remove the chocks from the wheels and spin the propeller for me. Make sure you stand back after each pull."

"I have propped a plane before." He placed the chocks to the side. The engine started on the first spin. He climbed into his seat and fastened his seatbelt tight around his waist.

Before he had time to grab the sides of the plane, the Jenny lifted into the sky as his stomach did a somersault. She flew around the farm and through town. His nerves settled, and he enjoyed gazing to the ground below. The engine was loud and the wind from the propellers kept his body glued to the seat. The whining of the wires lulled him as he relaxed, studied the simple gauges, pedals, and stick, and compared them in his mind to the Beechcraft Twin Beech. Aviation had sure come a long way in a short time. He would be an engineer and design ships; he'd never been more sure of anything in his life.

They arrived at the farm and Lisbeth guided the airplane toward the lake. His sense of security disappeared when the plane went into a barrel roll, a loop and roll done at the same time. He closed his eyes and willed his breakfast to stay in his stomach; his fear of heights reared its ugly head. One minute the sky was above him, and then the plane turned upside down with the ground below. She straightened the plane and flew in a circle before she did another. This time he kept his eyes open but clutched the sides of the plane, afraid his seatbelt would come undone and he'd fall out. She performed loops and a Cuban Eight. He settled in his seat and enjoyed the aerobatics as the smoothness of her flying and her skill for the tricks became evident. The plane approached the airfield and he didn't want the flight to end. The plane touched down in a perfect three-point landing.

The engine stopped, and she climbed to the ground. "Would you like to fly the Jenny?"

He considered for a moment but realized he'd never possess the flying skills she had. Not many men did. "No, I'll leave the Jenny to you and Frankie." He climbed out of his seat and helped her push the bi-plane to its hangar, placing the chocks under each wheel. They positioned the tarp over the seat openings and tied it securely.

He removed her hat and goggles, untied her scarf, and pulled her toward him with the ends. "You are one hell of a pilot, Lisbeth Rose." The gentle kiss he placed on her lips turned into a frenzied one, each trying to get closer to the other. He wished they were at the hotel in Atlanta. He regained control and held her close. "I'm ready for lunch, are you?"

She gathered their hats and goggles and her scarf. "I'll get the food from the icebox. Let's eat at the picnic table."

He moseyed over to the wooden table and bench that sat under a large oak. He wiped the bench with his handkerchief. A slight breeze made the heat of the day tolerable. Birds sang, and the occasional bee flew around, along with the sound of a passing car every now and then.

Lisbeth joined him with their sandwiches and a bottle of soda. "Ma made us ham salad sandwiches with tea cakes for dessert." She spread a large red-and-white-checked napkin over the table and placed the food before them.

He ate the sandwich. "Delicious, I've never had ham salad. Lillian makes a good chicken salad."

She wiped her mouth with a napkin. "I can't wait to meet her. She sounds delightful."

He finished his lunch and waited for her to take the last bite. "Wanted to talk to you regarding the test pilot job."

"What about it?" She faced him.

The determined expression on her face told him to tread lightly. "Are you sure you want this? There are other ways to use your skills."

She set her bottle on the table and waited a minute before she spoke. "I have weighed all my options. Before Victor married Dottie, he wanted to be an airline pilot, or thought he did until he realized he'd rather have Dottie and a family than travel all the time like your father does. Frankie always said an airline pilot was no more than a glorified taxi driver, and I have the same view. I'm not downplaying their jobs; we need good safe pilots."

"There are other jobs," he interrupted.

"I love teaching and flying people around and even love working as a mechanic, but the opportunity to fly the new ships as a test pilot and give advice as to how to make things better, that's what I want."

"All I care about is your safety." He held her hand and gazed in her eyes. The image of her crashing in a test plane brought physical pain to his belly.

She touched his cheek. "I know you do. But sometimes I wonder if my brother regrets not following his dream. I know he loves his family, but I think he could have been an airline pilot and a husband and father." She cradled his face with both her hands. "I may not get this job, but I'll give it my best shot."

He ended the conversation. Her stubbornness and determination were the qualities he admired. She hadn't said anything outright but made it clear he had no right to tell her what to do.

Chapter Eighteen

Paul drove through town headed to Andrews Field for the flight to Wichita. Since she'd told him her plans, he'd worried about her taking the job. He figured Edward Miller would hire her. Ed couldn't resist a pretty face, and with Lisbeth's skills, she'd make a damn good test pilot. If he wanted any kind of future with her, he'd have to relinquish his desire to control her. But, damn, he couldn't stand to think of anything happening to her, either.

He turned in to the parking lot and the gang circled around his airplane. Al pumped gas into the tank while Lisbeth and Frankie walked around the plane with the checklist. Victor stood on a ladder and cleaned the windshield.

He exited the car and retrieved his suitcase from the trunk. "Good morning."

She welcomed him. "I rode with Victor. We got here early to get the airplane ready, so we could leave as soon as you arrived."

He placed his suitcase in the Twin Beech. "Glad we have a good day for flying. Have you checked the weather in Wichita?"

"Called when I got here. No problems there."

The men shook his hand and hugged her; each gave her words of encouragement.

Al handed her a rabbit's foot on a chain. "This is

for good luck, Missy. I know you'll ace it."

She kissed Al's cheek. "Thank you."

He stepped back and grinned; his eyes brimmed with water. "Have a good flight, you two."

She climbed to the co-pilot spot, adjusted her seat, and fastened her seatbelt.

Paul studied the sheet attached to the clipboard. All tasks done and checked off. "Appears you guys did everything." He started the engines and entered the runway. The airplane lifted into the air. "You can fly a while if you want."

She straightened in her seat and took the controls. "How lucky you are to fly this plane every week. It's like flying in a dream ship."

He didn't know if it was her doing what she'd dreamed of or the fear of losing her in a crash or to another man, someone stronger and more handsome than him. He had to come clean with her. "It's a wonderful airplane and any pilot would love to fly it, anyone except me."

She checked the instruments and headed toward Kansas. "What do you mean anyone except you?"

"My father pressured me into this job, and I resent him…I resent him for a lot of things." He turned toward her, and their eyes met. "I envy you sometimes."

"Why?" she whispered. "You have everything. More than me."

"No, you have everything. You're not afraid to follow your dreams. Hell, most men wouldn't do what you do."

She concentrated on her flying. "Tell me what you want and why you don't think it's possible."

He studied the gauges to make sure the plane flew

in the correct direction. "I want to work in the field I trained in. I want to design new ships, make sure they're safe and up to date with the newest technology. Aviation's come a long way in the last twenty years."

"What's holding you back? You've got the education for it."

He was quiet for a long time. His voice rose over the sound of the engines. "I was pretty rebellious in college before mother died. I wanted to break free of their control. They chose my friends and my girlfriends, trying to mold me into the person they wanted. I wasn't interested and brought home girls they didn't approve of."

She interrupted him. "You sound like my sister, Ruth Ann; she did the same to my mother."

He continued. "When mother died, I realized what I'd done, and I was sorry I hurt her. I pleased my father by doing what he wanted instead of what I wanted. I've regretted it."

"Well, for God's sake, follow your dream. Don't listen to him or to any one, for that matter." She spoke over the engine noise. "If I listened to my mother, I'd be married with kids, living down the street from her, worrying about where we'd get the money to buy food and pay our bills." She glanced his way. "I think while we're in Wichita, you need to talk to someone about a new job yourself."

His belly rolled with excitement. "Maybe I will."

"No." She put her hand on his leg. "You will."

The rest of the flight, they concentrated on the flight plan. For the first time in a while, he dared to dream of the life he wanted and planned who he'd talk to when they landed. Maybe Cessna would hire him and

Lisbeth. If she wouldn't marry him, at least he'd live close. He would make damn sure the planes she flew possessed no design flaw.

She landed the plane like the seasoned professional she was. He pulled her close and kissed her mouth. "Good luck, sweetheart."

She placed her hand on his cheek. "Thank you." She unfastened her seatbelt. "I'll take a taxi to Cessna headquarters for my meeting, but where will I meet you?"

He wrote down the name of a restaurant. "Tell the taxi to take you to Edna's Diner. I'll meet you there after my meetings."

She put the paper in her purse. "See you then."

****

He strolled into Beech Aircraft offices. "Good afternoon. Is Mr. Reynolds in?"

The receptionist picked up the phone. "Yes, Paul Williams is here to see you. I will, thank you." She replaced the receiver. "You can go on back."

He headed to his boss' office with his briefcase in tow.

The meeting lasted thirty minutes. He received his instructions for the next two weeks and Mr. Reynolds approved his time off for the air race.

He left in a taxi toward Cessna offices. He'd request an interview with Hugh Burton regarding an aircraft engineer position. He'd go to Hugh's office in the front of the Cessna building and her interview would take place in the office close to the hangars and runway. He entered the familiar building.

"Here to see Mr. Parks?" The receptionist acknowledged him and smiled.

He hesitated. "No, Hugh Burton, if he's in."

"Can I tell him what this regards?"

He stuttered. "I…I want to talk to him about a job."

"Of course." She lifted the phone receiver and informed Mr. Burton he had a visitor. She placed the receiver on the cradle. "He said to come on back."

He walked toward the office. "Thank you."

Mr. Burton stood as he entered. "Take a seat." He shook his hand. "Good to see you. I'd ask how it is at Beech Aircraft, but since you requested a job interview, we'll table that."

He sat in the chair in front of the desk. "I have no problems with Beech, and Malcolm is keeping me busy selling airplanes. I'm grateful for the job there, they've been nothing but kind, and the pay is excellent."

Hugh Burton settled in his seat. "If that's the case, why are you in my office?"

He rubbed his palms together and remembered the speech he'd prepared. "Mr. Burton, I graduated from the University of Kansas School of Engineering with John Parks. Our goal was to work together designing new ships."

The manager folded his arms. "John's one of the best engineers I've ever hired. I had no idea you had an engineering degree. Why'd you choose the salesman job?"

He spilled his gut. "I listened to my father. He flies for Trans World Airlines."

Mr. Burton interrupted. "I know who your father is."

He picked up the contempt in the man's voice. Most people didn't like his father. They tolerated him because of his mother and her social connections.

"Well, he wants me to follow in his footsteps. He advised me to take the job at Beech Aircraft and hone my skills before I apply with Trans World. Honestly? I'm an engineer at heart, not a pilot."

The man opened a drawer and pulled out a bundle of papers. "Fill out the application and include all the information about your degree so we can get in touch with the university. I'll do what I can for you, but not promising anything. We don't need an engineer at the moment but won't say a definite no until I talk to my manager." He handed the papers to Paul. "You can sit in the waiting room and leave the application with the receptionist when you're done. I hope it works out for you."

He stood and shook Mr. Burton's hand. "Thank you, sir."

He filled in the information and surrendered the papers to the receptionist. "Please see Mr. Burton gets this."

"Of course. Best of luck to you." She took the clipboard.

He wanted to say hello to John, but his urge to see Lisbeth beckoned, and he didn't want Hugh Burton to think he was bothering the help. He called for a taxi and rode to the diner. A peace filled his chest as it did on the day he received his diploma with all the hopes and dreams his education brought, until his father destroyed it.

Chapter Nineteen

Lisbeth sat in the booth and recalled the interview. She remembered every word of their conversation. She stood her ground and didn't let him intimidate her. He tried his best, but she'd faced tougher adversaries. After she ignored his sexual advances and let him know what she expected from him as an employer, he settled into his seat and asked questions about her experience as a pilot and mechanic.

Paul entered the restaurant, and she stood and motioned him to the table.

He kissed her cheek. "How'd it go?"

She signaled the waitress. "Well, when I didn't respond to his flirting and he found out Frankie Howard taught me to fly and trained me as a mechanic, he got down to business with the interview. Said he'd hire Frankie in a minute."

He ordered a cup of coffee. "Yes, he's a ladies man, or thinks he is. Would Frankie consider the job?"

"I'll mention it, but I don't think he'll leave Saplingville. He's found the family he always yearned for, and I doubt he'd leave Al, Ethel, and my parents. Ruth Ann would follow him to the ends of the earth, I know that for sure."

"So do you feel good about it?" He added cream and sugar to his cup of coffee.

She placed her hand over her cup to signal the

waitress she was done. "Yes, I do. I told him Frankie and I would fly in the air race. That impressed him, and I think winning the race will seal the deal."

He settled his cup in the saucer. "You've got lots of competition, present company included."

She grinned at him. "Yes, I look forward to the competition. Will I meet John Parks while I'm here?"

He drank a sip of coffee. "Doubt it; I don't want to share you. The more people at the house, the more time I lose with you."

A shock wave pierced her lower belly when she remembered their weekend in Atlanta. They'd not been intimate since then, and she couldn't wait to lie in his arms. If they didn't make love again soon, she'd explode from desire. She whispered, "Will we be alone in the house?"

"Yes, unless my father is home, which I doubt. Even when he's in town, he has his hangouts."

She wasn't sure she understood. "Hangouts?"

He lowered his voice. "My father has women friends; he...um...well, he's a womanizer, always has been. He cheated on my mother for years; he hid it best he could, but everyone knew, including my mom."

A pain went through her heart. How much was Paul like his father? Would he grow tired of her and find another girl to fill his needs? "I'm sorry your mother had to endure such a life."

"Yeah, me too. Ready to go?"

She stood and opened her purse for her money.

He put his hand on hers. "I've got this. Find us a taxi."

By the time he paid and gathered his bag, she had the taxi waiting in front of the diner. He opened the door to the taxi and gave the driver the address.

Wichita reminded her of Atlanta with the tall buildings, wide roads, and traffic. "What a lovely city." The taxicab headed out of town on a two-lane road. Large houses with lush grounds lined the street. "A lot of rich people live in this town."

He said, "Uh-huh," and kissed her hand.

The taxicab turned down a paved path, too narrow for a road. "Is this a street?"

He smiled at her. "No, it's the driveway to the house."

The trees on each side nestled the car into the drive. The forest opened, and a mansion came into view. Flower gardens surrounded a large two-story house with wide steps leading to the most beautiful home she'd ever seen. "This is where you grew up?"

"Yes, this is home."

The driver opened the door and helped her from the car. She stared at the scene before her taking in the beauty of the house nestled in the pristine landscape.

A man shuffled from the flower garden, holding hedge clippers.

Paul hugged the man. "Wilfred Harper, this is Lisbeth Douglas. She's the lady flyer I told you about."

She gave the gentleman a smile. "Mr. Harper. It's very nice to meet you."

The gardener tugged off his glove and shook her hand. "Nice to meet you, Miss Douglas."

"Please, call me Lisbeth."

"And you can call me Wilfred."

Lillian Harper barreled down the front steps. Paul hugged her and lifted her feet off the ground. He placed her down and steadied her. "Lillian, this is Lisbeth Rose

Douglas."

Mrs. Harper hugged her. "Lisbeth Rose, what a beautiful name. I've heard wonderful things. I feel like I already know you."

She hoped he hadn't told them everything. "Yes, he told me about you two, also."

Lillian grabbed Lisbeth's suitcase. "Come in, I'll show you to your room, so you can freshen up. How did your interview go?"

She followed the woman to the porch. "He told you about my interview?"

The housekeeper opened the front door and stepped aside for her to enter. "Yes, he's very proud of you. We haven't seen him this excited about anything or anyone since his mother got sick and died. You've made quite an impression on him."

She loved the old woman right off. It was obvious she cared for Paul. "He's a very nice man; obviously you had something to do with his raising." She followed the woman up the stairs.

Mrs. Harper paused at the door to a bedroom. "He takes after his mother; she was a wonderful, kind and caring person. But, yes, Wilfred and I never had children and we've always loved Paul like a grandson. Here's your room; the bathroom is across the hall. Feel free to call on me for anything you may need. Dinner is at seven."

She surveyed the room. The ceilings higher than any she'd seen made the room appear large. The exquisite yellow wallpaper had a turquoise ribbon and bow design. A door painted with pink roses with a yellow background drew her attention. Her house in Saplingville didn't have closets in the bedroom. They used chifforobes for their clothes. She opened the door and found a bar with hangers for her dresses. A turquoise vanity table with a beveled mirror and a plush pink velvet chair sat next to the window. She sat in the chair and ran her hands over the smooth wood and opened the top drawer. It was empty except for a tortoise hairpin. Her reflection in the mirror stared back at her. She patted her cheeks with her hands to make sure this day was real. She hung her dresses in the closet and placed her powder box and lipstick on top of the vanity.

The four-poster bed with a solid turquoise bedspread beckoned. She fell on the bed and closed her eyes, afraid if she opened them, she'd be back in her room in Saplingville. Her father told her there was another world outside their little town but until now, she hadn't known what he meant. She sauntered to the window and surveyed the surroundings. Her bedroom was on the back of the house and she could see the carriage house the Harpers lived in. The cottage appeared small but well cared for, and rose bushes grew on trellises on each side of the entrance.

She peered down the hallway; it was larger than her bedroom at home. The only room with an open door besides the bathroom drew her. *Paul's bedroom.* She had to see the bed he slept in, so she could dream about it when she returned home. She stood at the door, afraid to enter. The furniture was a dark wood, with red-and-gold wallpaper. Two chairs surrounded the fireplace and bookshelves lined the wall on either side. The books lured her into the room. She studied the bindings and titles and ran her hands over the expensive book spines. She bought cheap paperbacks or borrowed books from the home town library. He had shelves dedicated to books by F. Scott Fitzgerald, Virginia Woolf, Ernest Hemingway, and Agatha Christie. She picked up *Women in Love,* by D. H. Lawrence.

"You can read any of the books you want."

The book fell out of her hand and she caught it before it hit the floor. "You scared me to death."

He stepped closer and pulled her into his arms. "It's a good book. You might learn something." Their lips met in a hungry kiss. He whispered in her ear, "I think you already know everything in the book."

Her face heated, and she turned to put the book on the shelf.

"No, this must interest you or you wouldn't have chosen it. Take it. He's a great author." He gave her another book. "After you're done, read the next one he wrote, *Lady Chatterley's Lover.* You won't find this book in any bookstore."

She studied the cover. "How did you get it?"

He gave her a smug smile. "A college bet and a lot of money got me this book."

He whispered in her ear, "You rest and read your books. After dinner Wilfred and Lillian will retire to the cottage and we'll have the entire house to ourselves."

Her heart beat in overtime and her core pulsated with hunger. "I'd love a bath to freshen up."

He led her out of his room to the hall. "Of course, there are towels, soap, and anything you need in the linen closet." He opened the door and handed her the toiletries. "I'll come back up a little before seven and escort you down."

She retrieved her bath robe and tiptoed into the bathroom. The tub was larger than their claw-foot at home and was built into the wall. She dropped her clothes on the plush fainting couch. She'd never seen a bathroom large enough to hold a sofa, stool, and chair. The tub even had a shower; she wouldn't have to wash her hair bent over the sink. She filled the tub with warm water and plunged herself in. She let the warmth surround her shoulders and neck and willed the tension of the interview away.

A knock on the door pulled her from the spell of the sexy book she'd devoured since her bath.

He opened the door and peered in. "Ready for dinner?"

She crossed the room and kissed his cheek. "I am. Is it just the two of us?"

"Yes, Father is out of town. Lillian says she expects him tomorrow."

The housekeeper greeted them at the door to the dining room. "Food's on the sideboard. If you need anything, ring the bell. I'll be in the kitchen."

He handed her a plate. "She made my favorite meal, roasted chicken, green beans, and potatoes boiled in butter."

She put a slice of chicken on her plate. "Looks delicious."

He pulled out the chair for her and poured white wine into her glass before he prepared the meal on his plate.

He sat at the head of the table and grabbed her hand. "I'll say a blessing."

She bowed her head and stared at the food and the beautiful dining room. She echoed his amen. "I feel like a princess; your home is spacious and beautiful. I've never been waited on before. Should I offer to help

Mrs. Harper clean up the dishes after we eat?"

He let out a quiet chuckle. "It's her job. She gets paid to take care of us."

"But she loves you like family."

"She does and so does Wilfred, but they are very proud people and they love their work; let them do it."

She cut a piece of chicken. "I see your point, although I've never had anyone do anything for me and I always helped Ma and Pa with chores around the house." She savored a bite of the meat and closed her eyes as it melted in her mouth. "So juicy and flavorful."

He whispered, "I could say the same about you."

"You'd better behave, mister." She raised her glass.

He tapped his glass in a salute. "Here's to new beginnings."

Their eyes locked together as the cool liquid entered her mouth and tantalized her senses.

When she ate her last bite of dinner, Lillian appeared as if by magic with a tray filled with a coffee service and two small plates of buttermilk pie. "I hope you saved room for dessert." She replaced their dinner plates with the pie and poured coffee into china cups. "Enjoy."

Lisbeth tasted the pie. The smooth confection melted in her mouth, the flaky crust perfectly baked. "Oh, my goodness, this is delicious." She savored the pie with the hot coffee. He hadn't taken even a bite of dessert. "What's wrong? Don't you like buttermilk pie?"

He put his hands in his lap. "Seeing you enjoy gives me more pleasure than dessert."

She handed Paul his fork. "Eat your pie."

"Yes, ma'am." They finished their dessert and drank another cup of coffee, making small talk. "Let's go in the library for sherry; I remember how you loved it at the restaurant in Atlanta."

She stood and put her napkin beside her plate. "Library? You don't keep all the books in your room?"

He put his arm around her waist and guided her toward the front of the house. "You're going to love this."

The large room held floor-to-ceiling bookshelves, plush sofas, two writing desks, and a large fireplace. "I never realized your father was so wealthy." A tense movement passed through the muscles of his jaw as if he wanted to say something but held back. "I'm sorry, I've never been in such a house before, and I didn't mean to talk about your father or his money. I'm sure he worked hard for it."

He poured her a glass of sherry and led her to a comfortable settee. "This has always been home to me. I can show you lots of nicks and scratches I made in the house, not to mention the broken vases and lamps."

She drank the sweet wine and let the liquid dance on her tongue. "Glad to hear you grew up like other little boys. I'd hate to think you had to sit here and read books during your entire childhood."

Lillian entered the room. "If you two don't need anything, Wilfred and I will retire to the cottage."

She stood. "Thank you for the delicious dinner. The pie was the best I've ever had and the chicken so juicy." She babbled nervously, hoping the old lady didn't suspect she'd spend the night in bed with Paul. "What time is breakfast?" *Well, that was about the stupidest thing I could say.* "Not that I'm hungry now."

Oh, good grief. "I'm not used to people feeding me and cleaning up after me, and I wanted to say thank you so much for everything you did for me today."

Lillian crossed the floor and hugged her. "Child, you are welcome. It's my job to take care of this family and I love every minute of it. You have a nice evening, and we'll see you in the morning."

He sat on the sofa with his hand over his mouth trying to hide his laughter.

She balled her fist and hit his upper arm. "Shut up."

He tugged her close. "You are adorable."

Chapter Twenty

The back door closed, the lock clicked, and he tugged Lisbeth to his lap. He turned her face to him and lowered his lips until he met hers in a gentle kiss. Weeks had passed since he'd made love to her the first time. He'd taken lots of cold showers and spent many sleepless nights without her in his bed. "I've missed you." He cupped her breast. He could feel the tautness of her nipple through her thin dress.

She let out a soft sigh. "I missed you, too."

He trailed kisses up her neck and sucked the lobule of her ear. "You smell like roses."

"So you like my perfume?"

"Uh-huh." He traced kisses down her neck and kissed the mound of flesh which begged for escape every time she took a breath.

She raised his head and placed her lips on his. He opened to her kiss; the sherry on their tongues mingled. If he died this moment, he'd know what it was to love a woman, and he loved her more than his life. "Go upstairs and get ready for bed. Lillian has your bed turned down and ready. Get in and make the bed appear slept in, and then come to my room. I want to make love to you in my bed." Her hands trembled in his. "Is something wrong?"

"No, I'm nervous and excited, it's been an amazing day with my interview, seeing where you grew up, meeting Lillian and Wilfred, and now getting to…" She wrung her hands together.

"Getting to be loved the way you should be loved…always." He put his arm around her, led her up the stairs and stopped at her bedroom door. "Don't be long."

"I won't." She took off her clothes as he closed the door.

He draped his clothes on a chair and scattered several prophylactics on the nightstand. If he had his way, he'd use them all.

She stood at the entrance to his room in a peach lace and silk night gown. The lace strained to keep her luscious breasts from tumbling out. She wore no shoes and her toenails sported polish the same color as her gown. He had a strong urge to suck her big toe into his mouth. He'd never done that to a woman, but it seemed appropriate with her. Hell, everything seemed appropriate with her. "You are a vision of loveliness."

She closed the door.

He rose to meet her. "No need to close the door. No one's here but us."

"I know, but I'll feel better if the door is closed."

"I understand." He pulled her close, her nipples pebble hard against his bare chest. He ran his hands over the silky material while he claimed her lips and crushed her close until they melted together.

She unbuttoned his undershorts and tugged them down to the floor.

He stepped out of them. "Not fair. If I'm naked so are you." He raked the hem of her gown until he had the entire lower half in his hands and pulled the garment over her head. "That's better. Any special requests, or shall I ravage your body as I like?"

She gave him a sheepish grin and her face reddened. "You remember the first thing you did to me at the hotel? It was the first time I...the first time I..."

He placed her on the bed, anxious to kiss every inch of her body. "Sweetheart, I remember." He pleased and explored his woman. She was his and he was hers, always.

Memories of their first night together flooded back. It was as if he'd never made love to anyone except her. She erased all memories of Kathleen and the girls who came before. Her smell, soft hair, delicate skin and eager lovemaking overpowered him. He wanted so desperately to say the three words on the tip of his tongue. "Lisbeth, I...I..." *Don't tell her, she'll bail.*

She raked her hands through his hair. "Yes?"

"I love making love to you." He nibbled on her neck.

"I love making love to you, too." She pulled him close and kissed his mouth.

He snuggled her body close to his. She was a perfect fit against him.

****

He woke and checked the time. Six eleven. He had approximately fifty minutes until Lillian opened the back door at seven. He kissed his love on the cheek.

She stirred and opened her eyes. "Is it time to get up?"

"Not yet. We have a few minutes." He pulled her into his arms, his tiger, eager and ready as him. Their familiarity with each other improved their lovemaking. Gone was the shy inexperienced girl. This morning, she led him places he'd never been. "Geez, Lisbeth, you've been reading the sexy book. Holy shit."

She gave him a wicked smile. "You like?"

"Hell, yeah."

They lay spent, snuggling under the sheet. The back door opened and closed louder than normal, signaling the housekeeper's arrival. He glanced at the clock, seven in the morning. "Time to get to your room and pretend you've been there all night."

She jumped up and grabbed her gown. "Will she come up here?"

He patted her butt as she skedaddled from the bed. "No, breakfast is served at eight. I'll come by your room and get you." He watched as she wrapped the gown around her body and raced from the room.

Paul knocked on her door. "Ready for breakfast?"

"I'm starved." She strolled toward the stairs.

He stared at the back of her head. She'd put her hair in a French braid, and he longed to release it and run his fingers through the silky strands.

"Good morning." Lillian breezed past them with a bowl of scrambled eggs and set it on the dining room table. "I hope you had a good sleep."

"We did." He pulled out a chair and winked at Lisbeth. "We have to leave this morning. I hoped to stay a few more days, but I checked the weather and a storm is coming in tomorrow."

The housekeeper placed a silver toast rack on the table along with strawberry jam. "I hoped you could stay, too."

Lisbeth returned her coffee cup to the saucer. "I've enjoyed meeting you and your food is so delicious. Thank you for everything."

Lillian poured more coffee in Lisbeth's cup. "You

are welcome, my dear. See that he brings you back soon."

He placed jam on his toast. *If I have my way, she'll be here all the time.* He imagined how his life would change with her as his wife.

"I'll let you two enjoy your food." She turned to go. "Ring the bell if you need me."

"She's so sweet, she reminds me of Aunt Delores." Lisbeth ate a bite of cantaloupe.

"Yes, she does. Both women love to feed people." He stared at the newspaper beside his plate; usually he read the daily news while he ate but not today. His girl would get all his attention.

She refreshed their coffee. "You checked the weather here and all the way home?"

He gave her a sly smile. "You sound disappointed."

A blush formed on her face. "I would have liked to stay another night. I wanted to see what Mrs. Harper would serve for supper."

"Is that the only reason?" Her smile melted his heart. He placed his hand on hers and squeezed. "This has been an incredible trip; our lives will change drastically if we get the jobs. Are you ready?"

She wiped her mouth with her napkin. "I'm overwhelmed when I think about working for Cessna. I'll have my dream job, but I have to give up my family and a life I love. I owe so much to Victor and Frankie and Al. How does it make you feel to think of leaving Beech Aircraft?"

Hope filled his heart. Hope for a life with her and a life doing what he chose to do not what his father chose for him. "Mother is gone, and Father, well, I'm my own man now. I'm leaving Beech whether I get the job or not."

"I hope if I have children, I can let them go when it's time. My mother couldn't do that for Ruth Ann and me."

A huge smile filled his face. "On our first date, you declared marriage and children not your goal in life. I'm happy to hear you are giving it more thought."

She folded her napkin and placed it on the table. "Guess I better get my things ready."

He stood as she did. "I'll call a taxicab."

They stood in front of the house with the Harpers and stacked their luggage in the trunk. A tear formed in Lillian's eye. He hugged her and whispered in her ear. "If I have my way, we'll both be back soon and never leave."

She said in a low voice, "Don't let her get away. She's perfect for you. Your mother would have loved her."

A deep red Cadillac coupe rolled down the drive. "Father's here."

The automobile came to a stop and Matthew Williams stepped from the fancy car. "Good morning, what do we have here?" He stopped in front of her and stared from the top of her head to her feet before he rested his gaze on her body.

Paul didn't like the way his father ogled his girl. She wasn't one of his tarts. "Allow me to introduce Lisbeth Douglas."

She put out her hand, but he pulled her into an embrace and let his hand rest on her lower back. Paul wanted to punch him. "We are on our way to the airport."

Matthew released her. "Sorry we didn't get a chance to visit." He winked at her. "Maybe next time."

They said their goodbyes and settled into the taxicab. Paul gave the driver instructions.

"Sorry about that," he apologized to her.

"About what?"

Lisbeth pretended nothing had happened, but he didn't miss how rigid she became when his father hugged her, and he saw the reservation on her face. He let the subject drop. Nothing would spoil his memory of the last two days with her.

Chapter Twenty-One

Lisbeth longed to take another hot bath in the large tub after Mr. Williams put his hands on her. He reminded her of a snake, and the way he raked his eyes over her body made her skin crawl. Everything Paul said about him was true. "I wish I could have met your mother." She said as she settled in the co-pilot's seat of the Twin Beech.

"I wish you could have, too. She was a good woman and a great mother. She spent a lot of time with me. I lived in the large house with no siblings. John lived in town and I loved to go visit and play with the neighborhood kids. When he visited, she put on her denim pants and played softball with us."

She glanced at him. "What a wonderful memory."

"My father made her life hell, but she made the most of everything. Held her head high and faced the gossip with dignity and grace." He stared out the window when the plane jerked and twisted. His grip tightened on the controls. "What the hell?"

"You know it's just turbulence. Frankie calls it a bump in the road. I got this." She stared at him, surprised at his response. Sweat broke out on his face. "Are you all right?"

He wiped his forehead with a handkerchief. "Yes, well, I do have a fear of heights." He relinquished the controls to her.

The flight smoothed, but once turbulence started, it took a little while for the skies to calm down. "I've read about pilots who don't like high places. They won't fly unless they're in charge of the airplane and have complete control."

He raised his hands. "I feel very comfortable with you flying. I don't care to wrestle with this today. I do it enough on my own."

She glanced his way and smiled. "Thanks for the confidence. Let's hope Cessna hires you and you won't have to fly around the country for a living."

"Yes, hope and pray." He flashed her a smile. "You're in charge for the remainder of the flight."

She landed the plane at Andrews Field, and the men met them, anxious for news.

Her brother greeted her with a hug. "How'd it go?"

Al and Frankie assisted Paul with the luggage and stored it in his car.

She grabbed her purse and clipboard. "Let's go to the hangar, where it's cooler." The stifling heat of the South caused her to sweat, and the sun burned her face. "I didn't miss the heat, I'll tell you. It's hot in Kansas but not as humid as here. I'll take dry heat over this sticky weather any day."

When they entered the hangar, Al passed out bottles of soda. "Missy, tell us what happened on your adventure. Did you get the job?"

She drank a swig of the cold liquid, making sure the bubbly drink went down. She'd die if she burped in front of her boyfriend. "Mr. Miller seemed interested. He said he had more people to interview and would let me know. If I get the job, it's because of you two." She smiled at her brother and brother-in-law. "He was mighty impressed when I told him I was taught by Frankie Howard and Victor Douglas. Said I must be good to be trained by a famous barnstormer and a military-trained fighter pilot."

Al raised his bottle in a toast. "The man thinks like me."

They clinked bottles. She continued. "Frankie, he said to tell you he'd hire you without an interview."

Her brother-in-law clutched the green bottle. "Mighty kind of him, but I'm not uprooting my family and leaving Saplingville. I've got it good here. Victor, Al, and I are a team." He nodded toward his comrades. "I'm the luckiest man in the world."

She watched Al brush a rogue tear from his face. The old man had a huge heart. "I figured you'd say that. I told him you weren't interested."

"It was nice of him to remember me." He took a drink of his cola.

She continued, "I told him we entered the air race. If we win, I think it might clinch the deal."

Victor added, "If you win? More like, when you beat all those bastards to the finish line." He glanced at Paul. "Sorry, man, didn't mean to call you a bastard. Just a figure of speech."

"No offense taken. I should call John and beg out of this race. We don't stand a chance against Frankie and Lisbeth." He stared adoringly at his girl.

"Nonsense. There are so many factors that come into play with a race. Anyone could win." Frankie added, "But we'll give you a run for your money, won't we, Lisbeth?"

She gave him a smile that lit up the dim hangar. "Got that right."

Al collected the bottles and placed them in the wooden box he used to transport the glass to the store for a refund. "I'm headed home. Y'all have a good weekend."

Frankie followed him. "Me, too. I promised to take my wife and son to the park for a picnic."

The boss turned off lights and made a last walk through and locked the door. He waved to his sister. "Congratulations again on your interview, sounds like you aced it."

"Thank you." She and Paul walked to his car.

He opened the door for her, and she slid into her seat. He bent down and gave her a gentle kiss on her mouth. "Man, I'm going to miss you."

She wished they were back in Kansas. "I'll miss you, too. Thanks again for letting me fly the Twin Beech and putting me up at your house."

"Sweetheart, the pleasure was all mine." He walked around to the driver side door and waved to Victor.

The drive toward town gave her time to decide how much to tell her parents. Her mind whirled from her private time with Paul to her interview, then jumped to the upcoming air race. They had to win; a job and money she needed for her move depended on the outcome. Paul could use the money, and his friend, John, hell, everyone needed money. They needed the dough as much as she did.

He held her hand. "You're quiet."

"I'm thinking."

"About what?" He made a left turn on her street.

She turned toward him. "So much has happened the last few days, I'm overwhelmed with my job prospect and excited about the race."

He turned in her driveway. "I want to spend time with you this weekend. I've got a full schedule of traveling and won't see you until the start of the air race in Miami."

Two weeks without seeing him? Her stomach sank like a rock thrown into Uncle Walter's lake. "Be careful and watch out for the holes in the road." A knock on her window interrupted them.

Hattie struggled to open the locked car door. "Lisbeth." Happiness that her daughter was home filled her voice.

She opened her door and stepped out. "Hi, Ma. We made it back safe and sound."

"We missed you."

She hugged her mother. "It was only overnight."

"I know." She retrieved the suitcase from the trunk.

He wrestled it from her. "I've got this, Mrs. Douglas." He let the ladies walk ahead.

She entered the house and motioned for the two of them to sit in the parlor. "You two sit on the settee and tell us all about the trip."

She folded her hands in her lap and began telling what she wanted them to know. Her father questioned her about the interview and Hattie ignored it like it never happened. She was more interested in where Paul lived and what his housekeeper served for dinner.

He stood to leave. "I'm exhausted, and I know Lisbeth is tired from her trip."

She walked him to the front door. "See you tomorrow?"

He raised her hand and kissed the back of it. "Yes, I'll call you in the morning and we'll make plans."

She gave him a sly grin. She wanted to take him upstairs and make love to him, but her parents would die of a heart attack. "I'll see what's playing at the picture show." She stood in the door until he got in his car and waved.

She turned; her mother waited outside the kitchen door. "Did they use silver and china at every meal?"

She followed her mother to the kitchen and drank the ice water she offered. "Yes, and the house is decorated like the pictures in *Better Homes and Gardens* magazine." She described the house and the rose garden and flowers Mr. Harper tended with care.

Her mother soaked in the information. "Sounds like his father is very wealthy."

"Seems so." She set her glass in the sink. "Need help with supper?"

Her mother shook her head. "No, I made soup. You want biscuits or cornbread?"

"With soup, I prefer cornbread." She turned to go to her room, and hesitated. She pulled her mother into a hug. "Thank you, Ma."

"For what?" Hattie stared at her with a surprised expression.

"For all the things you do for me."

"But I'm your Ma. That's what mothers do." She turned to get a bowl from the cabinet. "You go on and rest and I'll call you when it's ready."

She grabbed her suitcase and climbed the stairs to her room.

She unpacked and sniffed the silky nightgown. Paul's cologne lingered on the material. She was growing quite fond of him, but she blocked that truth from her mind; she had a job to claim, an air race to win, and a move from home to a strange town which needed her attention.

Chapter Twenty-Two

Paul sat at the desk in his bedroom at the boarding house, preparing his papers for the next two weeks. In a month's time he could have a job in Wichita, working with John. If all went his way, Lisbeth would have a job at Cessna also. They had to live in the same town. Being away from her for a week flying around the country was torture. He didn't know how long it would take to convince her to marry him. He'd never had to tiptoe around a woman before. Lisbeth Rose was special, and he loved every single thing about her. He hoped someday she'd love him enough to give up her independence she so desperately clung to. A rap at his door and Dottie's voice calling him to the phone broke his concentration. "Yes, Dottie, I'll be right there."

He eased down the stairs to the dimmed parlor and grabbed the receiver. "Hello, this is Paul Williams."

His father's voice filled the wire. "What's this I hear about you leaving Beech?"

"Yes, Father. I'm fine, and how are you?" He searched the dim room and listened for anyone within earshot. "Who told you?"

"Gossip travels fast in this town. Let's say I have my sources."

He lowered his voice. "Yes, I did talk to Hugh Burton at Cessna. It's what I should have done after graduation. That's the job I trained for, not flying around the country selling airplanes."

Matthew Williams responded, "I told you, you need experience if you want to fly for Trans World."

"Listen, Dad." He struggled to keep the animosity out of his voice. "I didn't stand up to you before, but I am now. I do not want to fly for Trans World Airlines. It's your dream. Leave me alone and let me follow mine."

His father ignored him. "And about the southern tart. I see why you are after her like a dog in heat and I hope you get a lot of nookie. Wouldn't mind having some myself, but she is not marriage material. Kathleen's father told me you haven't been seeing her when you come into town. You know he and I have an agreement. You are to marry her. And make it soon. You can see this girl on the side until you get tired of her."

Heat radiated from his face and rage caused his hand to shake. His voice came out in a monotone. "Stay out of my business; you have no right, whatsoever." He waited for a response, when nothing came, he said. "I want you out of my house, do you hear me? I want you to take your personal things and leave. Go live with your woman in town." The line went dead. He replaced the receiver on the cradle. He should have told his father to leave when the will was read. The lawyer advised him, but he'd hoped he and his dad could repair their relationship. He should have known better.

****

Paul and John sat in the outside restaurant at the Palm Hotel in Miami, Florida. Paul dipped the ice-cold shrimp into the horseradish-laden cocktail sauce. "After we're done with lunch, we'll head over to the airport

159

and check out maps and weather." He popped the crustacean in his mouth and savored the taste.

John tasted the appetizer. He made a face and swallowed the chewy meat. "I think this is a taste I haven't acquired yet." He guzzled water to wash the shellfish down and pushed his plate away.

Paul traded his empty glass with his friend's and finished off the shrimp cocktail. "Not something you would find in the Midwest. I've become addicted to it since I've been traveling to the coastal cities."

The waitress approached their table. "Ready to order your entree?"

John handed her his menu. "A hamburger, please."

Paul studied the lunch specials. "Bring me the crab cake plate."

She cleared their appetizer dishes and hurried to put in their order.

John leaned forward. "News is you talked to Hugh about a job with us at Cessna. You tired of flying cross country?"

He folded his arms across his middle. "I was tired of that job the first day. Not my cup of tea. You think I have a chance?"

"Well, I didn't think they needed another engineer, but Mr. Burton asked me about you; he seemed interested."

Paul sniffed the wine in his glass and drank. "I am grateful for the job at Beech because, if I'd refused the position, I wouldn't have met Lisbeth Rose Douglas."

"Kathleen thinks you're going to marry her."

He broke off a piece of French bread and smeared it with butter. "I have no intention of marrying her."

"And Lisbeth, are you going to marry her?"

"I want to, but she's not the marrying type. I hope to change that, though." He watched the ocean waves lap at the sand.

John lowered his voice so no one would hear. "Does she know about your inheritance?"

A sailboat drifted in the distance, he watched the occupants raise a sail. "Her career goals mean more to her than the almighty dollar. She's not into wealth and material things." He lowered his voice and stared at his friend. "She thinks the house and money belong to Father."

"When are you going to tell her?" The waitress placed a large plate with a hamburger and fries in front of John.

Another waitress presented Paul with lunch. He inhaled the crab cakes served with tropical slaw and fries. "When the time is right."

Chapter Twenty-Three

Lisbeth and Frankie arrived at the Miami Airport in the afternoon and locked and tied down their red Beechcraft Model D Seventeen Staggerwing with the planes of the other racers in the designated area. She noticed the yellow Staggerwing. Paul would fly a yellow one in the race; he could be here already. They entered the airport and headed to the restaurant. She searched every face in the crowd hoping to see him.

The waitress sat them at a table in front of the window so they could observe planes take off and land.

She studied the menu. "I'm so excited; I don't think I can eat anything."

Frankie placed his menu in the holder. "I know, but I learned a long time ago you need your nourishment because the rush you feel flying in a race takes a lot of energy. You'll perform better if you're not hungry. We'll take some apples and crackers and hard cheese along with us."

"Ruth Ann taught me the breathing technique she uses in her acting—I'll use that to keep calm—but damn, I'm so excited, I don't think I slept two hours last night."

The waitress placed two colas on the table and poised her pen on the pad for their order.

"I'll have the bacon, lettuce and tomato sandwich." She put her menu in the holder.

"Roast beef on rye for me." He stuck a straw in his glass. "There's a motel next door to the airport. It's better to stay close."

"I agree. We're not here to see the beach." She forced her sandwich down while Frankie enjoyed his along with icebox lime pie.

He ate the last bite of dessert. "You don't know what you're missing. Before we leave you have to get a piece of this."

"Maybe I'll have a slice tonight. What's the plan for the rest of the day?"

He picked up the tab and counted money out of his money clip. "Let's check into the motel, rest a while, and come back here and clean the airplane. We don't want any dust or dirt holding us back in the air. The cleaner the plane, the faster it'll fly."

They checked into their rooms and made a plan to meet in one hour. She splashed water on her face and lay on the bed, making a note of the time on the clock before she squeezed her eyes shut. She tossed to her back, then her other side; she was wide awake. She fidgeted for half an hour until she recognized Frankie's distinct knock.

She grabbed her purse and peeped out the window. "I'm ready to go." She made sure the door locked behind her.

"I had a nice nap, how about you?" Frankie walked beside her.

"I wish," she responded. "I'm too excited to sleep."

They walked the several blocks to the airport. She cleaned and polished the exterior while her brother-in-law kept his head in the engine. She cleaned the inside windows and polished the gauges. Not a speck of dust remained. "I think I'm ready for the icebox lime pie." She stored the rags behind the seat. She and Frankie had supper in the airport restaurant before heading to their rooms. The place was packed; she searched every table and Paul was nowhere to be seen.

****

Lisbeth and Frankie worked a re-run of the day before. She polished the exterior, removing any dirt. "The salt and sand seems to float through the air. I can feel the build-up since yesterday."

He wiped grease from his hands on a rag. "I hate Florida; the heat and humidity's worse than Georgia and the mosquitoes are bigger, too."

She ran a cloth under the airplane to clean the grime from the underside. Two men approached them, and she stood shading her eyes with her hand to block the sunshine. She recognized her boyfriend and another man she assumed was John. "Paul's here." She scrubbed her hands with the rag and stuck it in her pocket.

Paul embraced her planting a quick kiss on her lips. "Hey, angel. I've missed you."

"I missed you." She stood close to him and gave his companion a smile.

Frankie shook Paul's hand. "Good to see you."

"You, too." He motioned toward his friend. "John, meet Frankie Howard."

John put out his hand. "Man, this is a privilege to meet a real barnstormer."

"It's a privilege for me to meet a designer of new ships." The men shook hands.

The engineer stared at her. "It's great to meet you, Lisbeth. Paul talks about you all the time."

"I've heard good things about you. Glad to put a face with a name." She gave him a smile, but her eyes focused on her boyfriend.

"Me, too." He turned to Paul, nodded his head and winked.

She pointed toward the yellow Staggerwing. "Is that your plane?"

"Yes. It's a loaner from Beech." Paul stared at their plane. "I don't see even one speck of dust."

"Frankie says…"

Her partner cleared his throat. "Don't tell our secrets, Lisbeth."

She gave her brother-in-law a questioning glance; she realized John and Paul either didn't care about grime build-up or didn't care if they won the race. "Are y'all here for the meeting?"

"Yes." Paul reached for her hand. "Ready to go in?"

His touch caused electricity to flow through her arm. Their eyes met, desire evident in the gaze.

"Two weeks is too long to be away from you," he whispered.

"I agree." She shared a knowing smile with him. "How was your flight?"

They followed the two men inside the building. "No problems. Weather was perfect. Hope it stays good for the race."

She let her eyes adjust to the room. "I think we're late to the party."

The room was full of people. She and Frankie sat on the front row and Paul and John a few rows back. "How many entered, do you know?"

The barnstormer said in a soft voice, "There are

eighteen teams. I found a room where we can go over the maps one more time after the meeting."

"Good, I don't want to leave anything to chance." She turned and searched the crowd and spotted one female entrant. She nodded toward the lady and smiled.

The organizer got everyone's attention. "Good morning. Welcome to the Chambers Trophy Air Race. I take it everyone has signed in and filled out all the forms. If you haven't or have questions, talk to Elbert." He motioned to an older gentleman sitting behind him. "This is the time for you to ask questions, review the rules, and get acquainted with each other. It's a race, and whoever flies the fastest and navigates the route better than the next will win. We've factored in time for unfavorable weather conditions, so you'll have three days to make the trip. If Mother Nature cooperates with the race, you won't need the extra time. If there aren't any questions, meeting is adjourned."

She memorized everything the man said and studied the checklist. They did everything yesterday when they arrived but losing on a technicality was not acceptable. The energy in the room was palpable. Many of the pilots knew each other and told stories about their exploits.

She lost Frankie in the crowd. His flying buddies cornered him, and others stood in line to meet him. She couldn't believe after all these years people still remembered him and his flying skills.

Paul approached her with John by his side. "Want to have dinner with us tonight?"

"We need to study our maps and go over plans, but we'll have time when we're done. Where are you staying?" She hadn't seen them at their small motor lodge next door.

"We're staying at the beach. Where's your hotel?"

The lust on his face caused her core to contract. "We're next door at the Sands Motel, why don't we eat at the airport restaurant around six?"

"We could go somewhere fancier, my treat," Paul said.

The last thing she needed before the race was a fancy heavy dinner. "I'd prefer to eat a light supper and get to bed early. You know, early bird catches the worm, or wins the race." She smiled at her two competitors.

Chapter Twenty-Four

The alarm clock pulled her from a deep slumber. Worn out from the previous day's activities, she had managed to get some well-deserved sleep. She dressed and packed her small suitcase, her entire body vibrating from the excitement of the air race a few hours away.

She heard a knock at the door and Frankie's voice. "Lisbeth, are you ready?"

She opened the door; her brother-in-law held his bag and a taxicab stood near the curb. "Yes, ready to go."

He stuffed their suitcases into the trunk. "We'll have breakfast, check the weather, and go over the airplane one more time."

The cool morning air and the breeze from the ocean tantalized her senses. "It's a beautiful morning."

Frankie waited for her to enter the cab. "Yes, a great morning for take-off. I hope the weather in the entire state is calm."

The airport buzzed with commotion. Along with arriving and departing flights, the air race contestants milled around the restaurant, hangars, and airplanes. Well-wishers stood along the edge of the runways and people sat on the hoods of their cars parked along the road, waiting for the race to begin.

She lined their plane up in formation. They'd drawn the number four last night, so their red

Staggerwing idled, ready for the first three airplanes to go before them. The airplane seemed to have a mind of its own, not wanting to be held back from take-off. She got the go-ahead and their plane lifted into the air, the exact time noted in the timekeeper's log.

Frankie also noted the time in his book. "Here we go." He gazed out the window to the ground below. "Head east. We'll follow the iron compass to West Palm Beach and go west when the railroad splits, all the way to Georgia."

She nodded. "Got it." She commanded the airplane, leaving the other aircraft, which all seemed headed on a different path than theirs. "Guess everyone has their own flight plan."

"Seems that way." He studied a map and made notes.

They settled into a rhythm, both observing the ground and compass as they flew over the state of Florida. He kept watch for the iron compass and made a mental note of the locations of the airports in case they needed to land. He also checked her speed and made notes. "Great job; we've been cruising at around two hundred two miles per hour. At this rate and with luck, we could win this."

She concentrated on the flying; the red Staggerwing complied with her commands. She knew this airplane and it knew her. Frankie navigated them to Andrews Field. He radioed ahead and advised Al of their estimated time of arrival.

"I'll pee and we're back in the air as soon as possible." She relaxed at the familiar surroundings. Al stood ready to gas up the engine. Not until she exited the plane did she relinquish control to her overstretched bladder. She ran into the hangar to the restroom while the men checked over the plane.

Al wiped dust and dirt off the red airplane. "Victor, Jacob, and Ruth Ann flew to Cleveland yesterday. Said to tell you good luck and they'll see you in the winner's circle."

"We've got a good chance, I'd say." Frankie inspected the engine.

She ran to the Staggerwing. "Pee and let's go. Thanks, Al." She jumped into the plane, willing her body to stop shaking from nervousness. She could feel her heartbeat in every cell of her body. She closed her eyes and took deep breaths, counting to ten on the inhale and exhale.

Frankie climbed into his seat. "Al wrote down the weather forecast and warnings."

The airplane lifted from the runway. She checked gauges and settled in for the trip north. "Yes, he told me there's a front moving in. I think we can get ahead of it."

Frankie wrote down numbers, checked the map, and re-read Al's notes. "I agree. If we're lucky, we'll arrive in Columbia, South Carolina, before the storm grounds us. We'll spend the night there; it's half way to Cleveland."

He opened a paper sack and handed her a sandwich. "Potted meat and mayonnaise, compliments of Al."

She ate the sandwich but refused the water jug. "I'm not drinking anything. My bladder is the size of a pea."

He drank a large swig. "When we get to South Carolina, you must drink water. I can't have you dehydrated."

"I will, and I'll eat a good supper. Promise." She settled into the sway of the ship floating through the air and flew like her life depended on it.

Soon the clouds rolled around them, and the plane bumped through an air pocket, sending the log book and maps to the floor. "Careful." He checked gauges. "The storm's chasing our tail, but we can outrun it."

She continued to fly with determination and focus. "I've got this."

"If we stay ahead of the rain, we'll make it with no problems." He gathered his notes and stuffed the pen into the book.

The storm chased them all the way to Columbia, but they landed before the torrential rain started.

The manager of the airport, a Mr. McKenzie, greeted them. "You're the first to land. I think most of the racers got caught in the storm."

They ran to the part office, part hangar, the wind howled, and the rain beat in a steady stream. The manager pointed toward a door. "Ma'am, the bathroom is there if you need it."

She cursed her bladder but hurried to the restroom. "Thank you."

Mr. McKenzie signed the flight log to verify their time of arrival in Columbia. He called the race headquarters in Cleveland to report their location and the time they landed.

Frankie studied the weather reports. "What's the forecast for tomorrow?"

She entered the office, sat in a chair, and ran her fingers through her hair, loosening the damp curls.

"Supposed to clear up tonight. Ten percent chance

of rain tomorrow. I don't know where the other racers holed up, but I don't expect anyone else made it through the front. Y'all are damn lucky." The heavens opened up and rain pounded the tin roof, making it difficult to hear.

"Yes, we are." She smiled and let the knowledge they led in the race sink into her brain. "Is there a motel around here?" She spoke over the tumultuous sound of the rain.

"Sure is. Get your stuff and I'll drive you." He stood and retrieved his car keys from a drawer.

Frankie shook his hand. "Thanks, we'll get our suitcases."

The manager handed him an umbrella. "You'll need this."

Lisbeth held the cover over their heads. "I'll hold this; you get the luggage."

The wind blew a spray of water that soaked their clothes.

They stuffed their things into Mr. McKenzie's car and piled in.

She apologized. "Sorry for the mess we're making of your automobile."

"No worries, ma'am." Mr. McKenzie stopped his car in front of the motel. "It's not much, but it's close and clean."

"It's perfect." She retrieved her suitcase. "Can you pick us up at five in the morning? We want to leave at daybreak."

"Sure will." He shook Frankie's hand. "See y'all in the morning."

****

Lisbeth and Frankie sat in the airplane, waiting for

the fog to lift enough so they could take off.

"This is it," she said as she fastened her seatbelt. "If no other weather problems, we should make it to Cleveland today."

Mr. McKenzie radioed an approval for take-off and advised them he'd call race headquarters.

Frankie fastened his seatbelt and wrote in his log book their time of departure. "Let's do this."

"Roger that." She glanced out the window, said a silent prayer, and taxied down the runway. She flew the airplane like a demon while Frankie studied the ground, railroad tracks, and map. She hadn't relaxed since they started the race, and her neck and back ached from the strain. She paid no attention to the ground below or the perfect weather and cloudless sky. She didn't know if it was her desire to win or the wind that propelled the airplane forward. She took the Staggerwing to its limit amazed at her speed. With determination and focus, she concentrated on only one thing, winning the race.

He straightened in his seat and pointed. "I see the airport."

She let her body settle against the seat, but the tension wouldn't release until she found out their standing. She steadied her shaking hand and picked up the radio, requesting permission to land.

On the descent, they saw thousands of people in the stands surrounding the runway. By the time she landed and taxied the plane to a stop, people spilled out, running toward them. They exited the Staggerwing, but she couldn't see her partner. Well-wishers surrounded both of them. "Did we win?" A throng of people touched her, hugged her and shook her hand. "Did we win?" she shouted. "Are we first?" she yelled louder.

Victor pushed his way to the front. "Yes, Lisbeth, y'all won." He hugged her and kissed the top of her head. "I am so proud of you."

"Where's Pa?" Her gaze searched the crowd for her father's brown hat with the gold band.

"Ruth Ann is with him. They stayed in the stands." He led her to the bandstand.

Somehow, Frankie had managed to get to the stage before them. He picked her up and swung her around. "Lisbeth, you did it."

She wobbled when he put her down. "Hell, no, we did it. I couldn't have won without you. Thank you."

Mr. Chambers from Chambers Aeronautical approached them. "Congratulations, I'm Samuel Chambers."

"Frankie Howard." They shook hands.

She put her hand out. "Lisbeth Douglas. Pleased to meet you."

"The pleasure is all mine. You are the first team with a woman to win my air race. This is grand." He pushed them to the podium and stood between them. "Ladies and gentlemen," Sam began. "I am extremely pleased to announce Miss Lisbeth Douglas and Mr. Frankie Howard have won the Chambers Air Race." The master of ceremonies handed him a trophy. "I present this trophy to the two of you; you'll receive the five-thousand-dollar check at the award ceremony tonight. Congratulations." He handed the trophy to them and stepped away.

Frankie held the trophy with Lisbeth while the photographer flashed a picture. He spoke into the microphone. "Thank you, it was an honor to fly with Lisbeth, she is one hell of a pilot." He raised her hand toward the crowd. "May I present to you a woman with a daredevil spirit."

The crowd roared and clapped.

She stepped to the microphone. She smiled at the crowd and lifted the trophy over her head. The audience cheered and rose to their feet. . "I…uh." Her voice came out in a whisper. She cleared her throat and inhaled a deep breath. "Thank you." She nodded to the crowd. "I want to thank the women who followed their dream of flying and paved the path for me…and my brother-in-law, Frankie Howard and my brother Victor Douglas, who taught me and believed in me when I was barely able to touch the foot pedals of the airplane. I've dreamed of flying in an air race since I heard the nineteen twenty-nine Women's Air Race on the radio. I was ten years old, but I knew…I knew someday I would fly in an air race. Thank you." She stepped back, and the master of ceremonies continued talking to the crowd. They stepped off the bandstand.

Ruth Ann ran to her husband. He picked her up and planted a lingering kiss on her lips. She wished Paul could celebrate her win with a kiss. She checked the skies every now and then, searching for their plane.

Jacob Douglas pulled her into his arms and held her. He whispered, "I am so proud of you right now."

She loved the hugs her daddy gave. She melted into his soft chest, letting his embrace wash away her nerves and give her strength. "Thanks, Pa."

Ruth Ann gave her a huge smile. "You did it, kid." She hugged her sister and grabbed her husband's hand.

To Lisbeth's left, Matthew Williams stood with a young woman. She approached them. "Mr. Williams, good to see you." She stretched out her hand.

He ignored the gesture. "We hoped Paul and John would come in first, but I see they lost to a woman and a has-been barnstormer."

Emotions raced through her body. The excitement of winning and the scathing words from Paul's father made her dizzy. "I'm sorry you feel that way, sir."

"Oh, no matter." He pushed the woman toward her. "This is Kathleen Warren, my son's fiancée."

She stepped back and glared at the woman. She had brown curly hair, green eyes and looked like she stepped out of a bandbox. Exactly what she'd feared since she met Paul. *Son of a bitch.*

The man and woman walked away laughing.

She searched the crowd for her brother. She shuffled toward him, gasping for air. She put her hands on her knees and forced air into her lungs.

Victor stared at her. "What's the matter? Who were those people?" He steadied her.

"That was Paul's father and the woman is Paul's fiancée."

"Fiancée? I don't believe it for a minute." Her brother cut his eyes to the two people.

"Get me out of here, now." Lisbeth's voice came out in a breathy whisper.

Before he could whisk her off, Mr. Miller approached. "Miss Douglas, congratulations on your win. Still interested in the job?"

She regained her composure and held her head high. This was her day, she won, and no one would spoil it. "Yes, sir."

"Wonderful. We'll talk later about your start date and salary."

She shook his hand. "Thank you. Let me introduce

my brother. Victor Douglas, meet Edward Miller, Head Test Pilot for Cessna."

"Pleasure to meet you, although I'm not too happy about losing one of my best mechanics and flight instructors."

Ed shook Victor's hand. "Your loss is Cessna's gain."

Frankie approached the man. "Frankie Howard."

"I know who you are." The test pilot shook his hand. "I've got another position at Cessna. We could use a man like you."

He pulled his wife close. "We're happy in Saplingville. I appreciate it, though."

"Well, if you change your mind." He turned to Lisbeth. "We'll talk later."

She smiled but her eyes stayed on Mr. Williams and the woman. They stepped into a chauffeur-driven car. She tried her best to forget the encounter while her brother introduced her new employer to the rest of the family.

Jacob spoke to Ed. "I trust you will put my daughter's safety first and foremost."

"Of course, sir. As we do with all our test pilots. It was a pleasure to meet everyone. I'll see you at the awards ceremony tonight."

Other air racers arrived one after the other; she couldn't face Paul. "I want to leave. Did you get me a room?"

"Yes." Victor turned to the family. "Lisbeth wants to rest; I'm taking her to the motel, anyone else ready to leave?"

Frankie spoke for the rest of the family. "We all need to rest before the festivities tonight. Let's go."

They waited for two taxicabs to arrive.

The yellow Staggerwing approached, and Frankie said, "Paul and John will place sixth." He turned toward his sister-in-law. "Want to stay and see him?"

Sweat popped out on her face and the blood pounded in her ears. "No." She stepped into the taxi with her father and brother.

Chapter Twenty-Five

Paul landed the Staggerwing and spotted the red Beech tied down. "I wonder what Lisbeth and Frankie placed?"

John gathered his belongings. "Won't surprise me if they won. Those two aren't afraid of pushing the limit."

He agreed. "Yes, with Frankie's navigation skills and Lisbeth flying like a bat out of hell."

They walked to the stage; the master of ceremonies introduced the two and congratulated them on placing sixth.

He shook the man's hand and spoke into the sound system. "Thank you, it's an honor to place so high among the excellent pilots flying in the race." He stepped back and let John say a few words.

"It's been a fun race, one I am happy to have been a part of. Thank you."

They stepped off the stage and he addressed the man in charge. "By the way, who won?"

"The team from Georgia, Lisbeth Douglas and Frankie Howard." The man beamed. "It's making national news, a woman flying the race faster than any man."

"Where are they?" He searched the crowd.

"Why, they left pretty soon after they arrived."

"Do you know where they went?" He had to see

his girl, tell her how proud he was and celebrate this moment with her.

The man headed toward the next team that landed. "Said they'd see us tonight at the awards ceremony."

Chapter Twenty-Six

Lisbeth waited until she was alone in her room before she broke down. She set the trophy on the nightstand and buried her face in a pillow to muffle her crying. The physical pain of her heart breaking surprised her and brought her to the realization she loved Paul. She blamed herself for letting him steal her heart and lead her to believe he loved her. Well, never again. This was a lesson well learned. She sat up on the side of the bed and stared at the trophy. A chuckle escaped her lips and she laughed and cried at the same time. They won the race and she got a new job but found out her boyfriend was engaged. How ironic, she got everything she wanted but lost her heart in the process.

She fell asleep and didn't wake until the knock on the door and Ruth Ann demanding to be let in woke her. She opened the door and stepped aside. "What do you want?"

Her sister slipped in the door and stared. "Your eyes are swollen. Have you been crying?"

She went to the bathroom and splashed water on her face. She blotted the water with a towel. "You know the man and woman who came up to me at the airport?"

"That older man and younger woman?" Ruth Ann sat on the bed.

"Yes, he's Paul's father and the woman is Paul's

fiancée." Tears flowed from her eyes.

"I don't believe it. He's crazy about you." She stood to console her sister.

Lisbeth turned away and wiped her face. "I am so stupid."

"Who told you she's his fiancée?" She put her hands on her sister's shoulders and looked into her eyes.

"Mr. Williams told me when he introduced her. Deep down I knew he had someone, but I didn't want to believe it." She put her head on Ruth Ann's shoulder and cried.

She gathered her little sister in an embrace. "Cry, let it out. I've got you."

She let the tears fall. Water and snot ran down her face. "I'm ruining your dress." She sat in a chair, wiping her face and nose with the back of her hand.

"I brought your things, they're in my room. I'll get them and help you dress. I'll do your make-up, and no one will know you've been upset. Take a bath and I'll be back in thirty minutes." Ruth Ann headed to the door. "We won't let him ruin the happiest day of your life."

Chapter Twenty-Seven

Paul arrived early for the awards banquet, anxious to see his girl. She wore a black beaded dress with fringe along the bottom, a true vision of loveliness. The material clung to her curves and the fringe danced as she walked. Mr. Douglas and Victor escorted her toward the front of the room. He raced toward them. "Lisbeth. Congratulations."

She ignored him. Her father guided her to their table.

Her brother put his hand on Paul's chest. "She doesn't want to talk to you."

"Why?" Confusion filled his mind while he struggled to remember their last conversation. Everything was fine.

Frankie stepped beside Victor, his clenched fists at his side.

He backed away; they meant business. The two men walked toward the head table to join Mr. Douglas, Ruth Ann, Lisbeth, and Mr. Chambers. *What the hell just happened?*

John approached him with his father and Kathleen in tow. "Look who I found."

He kept his eyes on Lisbeth until Kathleen wrapped her arms around his neck and kissed him on the lips. The feel of her in his arms made his stomach churn. He pushed her away. "I didn't know you planned to attend."

"Of course." She kissed his cheek. "I wouldn't miss it. Sorry you didn't win."

He glared at his father. "I didn't expect to see you either."

"This was quite disappointing; what happened you didn't win? Did you get lost on the way?" He gave his son a smirky grin.

He stared at his father. "We got behind a storm and we did veer off course a time or two. The best team won."

"Huh, why am I not surprised?" He whispered in his son's ear. "You wanted that little floozy to win."

He raised his hand to strike his father. The older man smiled and begged for it.

His friend pulled him aside. "He's not worth it. Let it go. I've got something to tell you later. Humor them and get through the night."

The master of ceremonies asked everyone to find a seat. Kathleen wedged herself between him and John and sat at the table between them.

Chapter Twenty-Eight

The woman melted her body into Paul's. She looked like a snake slithering into a hole. When they kissed Lisbeth looked away and wiped a tear that dripped from her eye. The son of a bitch and his tart would not spoil her night. She was the first woman to win the Chambers Trophy and the first woman test pilot for Cessna. He could go to hell.

She turned her attention to Mr. Chambers and her family.

"Lisbeth, I can't tell you how happy I am you and Frankie won the race this year. It's national news, you know." He continued, "A barnstormer and a lady flyer, they'll talk about this for years."

She turned her focus on her success, but her eyes went to Paul's table. Their eyes met, a sad expression plastered his face. A waiter set a plate of food before her, Salisbury steak, mashed potatoes, and green beans. Her stomach refused to accept the nourishment.

Ruth Ann put a roll on her bread plate. "Eat, don't pay them any attention."

She ignored the wine and sipped her water. She picked at the food on her plate, every bite difficult to swallow.

The waiters cleared the dessert plates and coffee cups from the tables. Mr. Chambers approached the stage and announced third, second and runner-up teams and passed out certificates. "Now for the moment you've been waiting for. Miss Lisbeth Rose Douglas and Mr. Francis Jack Howard, winners of the nineteen thirty-nine Chambers Air Race."

The entire crowd rose to their feet in a standing ovation. She walked toward the stage and stumbled on the step. Frankie grabbed her arm to steady her. The moment was surreal as she floated to the microphone.

Mr. Chambers stepped back and handed them a check. She held the paper and stared at the crowd, the applause subsided. "Thank you." She spoke into the sound system as the crowd quieted and sat in their seats. "My pa is here." She nodded toward their table and her lips trembled while she forced a smile. She bit her upper lip and swallowed to gain control of her emotions. "I'm glad he's here to celebrate this moment with me. I know he didn't like it when I told him I wanted to learn to fly, but he let me try." She paused and gave him a smile. "He wanted me to go to college, but when I told him I wanted to work at Andrews Field he encouraged me. He's always encouraged me. Thanks, Pa." She faced the crowd. "I've had the best teachers, my brother, Victor, and my brother-in-law, Frankie. This is an honor for me, and I'll never forget this. Thank you, Mr. Chambers." She turned toward him and backed away, giving her partner room to come forward.

Frankie smiled at the crowd. "I am honored to stand before you tonight and accept this award with my sister-in-law. For those of you who think it's easy to win a race such as this, let me tell you. Lisbeth didn't decide yesterday she would fly an air race and win. She's worked hard, she continues to learn and study, logs flying hours every week, teaches flying, and flies air taxis. She can do aerobatics like no one I've ever seen; yes, the student has surpassed her teacher." He waited while the crowd chuckled. "And she's a hell of a mechanic. Thank you for this opportunity."

They stood at the front while people mingled around, shook their hands and congratulated them. She watched Paul leave with his father and friends. She put on a fake smile and chatted with her fans.

Chapter Twenty-Nine

Paul said goodbye to his father and Kathleen and hailed a taxicab. When they arrived at the hotel, his friend handed him a newspaper clipping. "What's this?" He unfolded the newspaper.

Mr. and Mrs. Hubert Warren are pleased to announce the engagement of their daughter, Kathleen Elizabeth, to Paul Louis Williams, son of Matthew Louis Williams and his late wife Marjorie Ann Williams.

He crumpled the paper in his fist. "Where'd you get this?"

"Kathleen gave it to me. You didn't know?"

"Hell, no. I didn't know." The crowd in the lobby stared his way.

John guided him to a chair. "Calm down."

He sat in a chair and put his head in his hands. "My father's behind this. I told him to leave the house, and he's getting back at me." He raised his head and stared at his friend. "Lisbeth knows."

"How would she know?"

"Somehow, they got to her, told her. That's why she won't talk to me." He sat straighter in his chair. "When she arrived at the banquet, she ignored me, and Victor said she didn't want to talk to me. He and Frankie acted like a couple of goons ready to beat me up."

His best friend advised, "Talk to her, she'll understand. Tell her you had no part in this."

He inhaled and let out a breath like a steam cooker. "You don't know Lisbeth. She's nobody's fool. I've lost her, I feel it in my gut. Son of a bitch."

****

Paul landed the yellow Staggerwing in Wichita on Monday. He taxied close to the hangar and shutdown the engine.

John unfastened his seatbelt. "You gonna be okay?" He gathered his maps and notebooks.

He searched for his belongings. "I'll make this right with Lisbeth if it's the last thing I do."

His friend walked around the plane with his luggage and books. "Good luck, man. I hope so. She's the best thing that's ever happened to you."

They entered the office and found the manager. He inspected the plane while they waited.

Paul opened a notebook and started writing. "I'm making a list of what I need to do, starting with a retraction from the newspaper. Going by there as soon as we're done here."

"Don't do anything foolish or something you may regret later."

He exhaled a heavy breath. "That ship already sailed; regrets are all I have right now. I handled her all wrong from the time I met her."

John stuffed his log book in his luggage. "Can I take you to the newspaper?"

"No, I'll call a taxi." He picked up the phone and told the operator to connect him.

The manager came into the office and Paul signed the paper on the clipboard. "Thanks."

"Congratulations on coming in sixth. Quite an honor with so many other great flyers."

He agreed with the man, but praise was the last thing on his mind. "Thank you for the compliment."

Paul threw his luggage in the back seat and stepped into the cab.

"Where to?" The driver asked.

"*Wichita Journal* newspaper offices, please." He continued to write his list of things to do this week. He had until Thursday night to accomplish his goals.

The cab stopped in front of the office. "Wait for me, and you can take me to my home."

"Sure." The driver turned off the engine and settled in his seat.

"Thank you. This won't take long." He shuffled into the newspaper office. He stopped at the receptionist desk. "I need to see the publisher, please."

"He's very busy; I can get one of the editors to help you." She tapped a pencil on the desk.

His hands fisted at his side. "I want the newspaper to print a retraction."

"Regarding?" She stood.

He cleared his throat. "An engagement announcement from last week's paper was published in error." He pulled out his wallet, ready to pay if needed. "I want it publicly retracted in Thursday's edition."

She picked up the telephone. "Susan Bishop will help you. Have a seat."

He ignored her and stood waiting until Miss Bishop arrived and led him to her office.

****

Paul sat in the taxi and gave the driver his home address. He scratched through the most important task on his list and wrote in the margin. *Retraction done.* He wished he could be a fly on the wall when Kathleen read the notice. The retraction would extricate him from any and all society functions and soirees, and that was fine with him. After meeting Lisbeth Douglas and living in Saplingville with real, honest and hard-working people, he didn't want any more of this high society shit.

The cab turned in his long drive. He stared at the tree-lined entrance; memories of riding his bicycle and roller skating down the lane played like a moving picture. A smile bloomed on his face; he pictured his and Lisbeth's children doing the same. He willed himself to believe he could fix this situation.

The driver stopped in front of the house. "Need help with your luggage?"

He gave the man money for the trip and a large tip. "I've got it. Thank you."

Lillian greeted him at the door. "We didn't expect you."

He gave her a peck on the cheek and hurried up the stairs. "I'm staying until Friday morning."

"I'll have your dinner ready at seven as usual." She spoke so her voice would carry up the stairs. "Anyone else joining you?"

"No, just me." He deposited his things in his room and headed to his father's bedroom. He opened the closet filled with clothes. He walked down the hall to the top of the stairs. "Lillian?"

"Yes." She entered the foyer.

"Have Wilfred bring up some boxes."

"Right away." She left to find her husband.

He stuffed as many of his father's clothes as he

could into the luggage stored in the closet.

Wilfred entered the bedroom and deposited boxes on the bed. "There's more if you need them." He turned to go.

He stopped and walked toward the old man. "I told Father to get his things out of the house, but I see he didn't. I need your help, if you don't mind."

The man stood still and gazed around the room.

"If you don't want to help, I'll do it myself. I should have followed the attorney's advice and told him to leave when the will was read. Mother didn't want him to stay here."

Wilfred opened a box. "What do you want me to do?"

In an hour, they had the personal belongings of Matthew Williams packed up and loaded on Wilfred's truck. He drove into town and deposited the boxes on the front porch of his father's longtime girlfriend and rang the doorbell.

Sandra Armstead opened the door. "Can I help you?"

He stared at the woman; she had to be ten years younger than his dad, slim and well dressed. "Is my father here?"

"He's flying the next few days." She stepped out on the porch. "What's all this?"

"These are my father's belongings; see that he gets them." He gave her an envelope. "Give him this letter." He studied her face as she bit her bottom lip and read the missive. "He'll stay with you from now on."

She glared at the boxes and luggage. "This is a mistake."

"No mistake." He smirked. "You won't live in my

mother's house after all." He turned to go.

The woman sat on the porch bench and put her head in her hands. He strolled to the truck, satisfied with his decision.

He returned home, went to his room, and studied his list. He scratched off "get father's belongings out of the house." In the margin he wrote *good riddance*.

****

Paul slept better knowing he had eliminated two poisons from his life. One of the hardest things he had to do this week was quit his job. He liked Malcolm Reynolds and he appreciated how they treated him at Beech Aircraft, but unless they had an engineering job for him, he was history. He ate his breakfast, grabbed his list, and headed to the Beech offices.

Malcolm Reynolds rose from his desk. "Congratulations on coming in sixth in the air race."

"Thank you, sir. We had tough competition." Paul sat in the chair in front of the desk.

"I don't think anyone had a chance against the Georgia team competing. They set a new record." He sat at his desk and puffed on his cigar. "How's the job going?"

"That's what I want to talk to you about." He shifted in his seat. "About my job."

"What about it?" The boss man tapped the ash off his cigar. "You need a raise already?"

"No, you've compensated me well. I need to terminate my employment." He hurried with his explanation. "This is a great company and you've been wonderful to work for, but this isn't what I want to do with my life. My father pushed me into this."

Mr. Reynolds studied him. "I see. Anything I can

do to make you stay?"

"I'd stay with Beech if they offered me an airplane designer position, so I can use my engineering degree." He hoped he didn't sound desperate.

"Different department, but I'll give you a recommendation, if they ask." He opened his desk and removed some papers. "You giving a two-week notice?"

He closed his eyes and breathed a sigh of relief, one more thing done. "No, sir. I hope you don't mind but I have to quit today."

The man stared at him, his eyebrows slinked over his eyes and his mouth turned down. "I've got customers standing in line to see the Twin Beech and I don't have another salesman." His voice grew louder. "You can't come in here and quit before I find someone."

Paul placed his checkbook on the desk. "About the Twin Beech."

His step was lighter as he exited the office and made his way to the mechanical side of the operation. He showed the mechanic his bill of sale and gave instructions for the detailing of his newly purchased Twin Beech airplane. He paid extra to have the ship ready by Friday morning. He prayed for good weather; he had to get to Saplingville and make things right.

He drove to the Cessna Aircraft Company and entered the front door.

The receptionist hung up the phone receiver. "Mr. Park's in his office, go on back."

"Not here to see John. Is Mr. Burton in?" He fiddled with the car key in his pocket.

She lifted the phone and dialed a number. "Paul

Williams is here to see you... Go on back." She gave him a smile. "Good luck."

He gave her a slight grin. *Guess everyone knows my business.* He made his way to the office and reminded himself the world would not end if he didn't get the job.

Hugh Burton shuffled books aside and walked around his desk to the office chair. He placed two chairs facing. "Have a seat."

"Thank you." He sat in the chair, surprised at the closeness of the seating. "I stopped by to discuss the engineering position. I quit my job at Beech Aircraft today."

Mr. Burton crossed his right ankle over his left knee and brushed lint off his suit pants. "This is good timing. Had a meeting this morning with the boss. He said to make you an offer. But first, I need to understand your intentions. You'll design ships, not fly them. Your father gave us the impression you wanted to fly commercial airliners like him."

He scratched the back of his neck. "Well, my father was wrong. I don't enjoy flying every day; my heart is with engineering. I promise John and I working as a team will design the best and most modern cutting-edge ships in the business."

The man stood and grabbed a paper and pencil. "Exactly what John said when we talked to him." He wrote something on the pad and handed the paper to him. "Here's what we can offer. I don't have to tell you not to compare salaries with anyone."

He stared at the figure on the paper. "This is quite generous."

"To be the best, you pay for the best." He sat at his

desk. "When can you start?"

He grabbed the chair arms, afraid he might float out from sheer elation. "Week after next, if it's good for you."

Mr. Burton handed him a clipboard. "Works for us. Fill out all these papers and drop them at the front desk." He shook his hand. "Welcome to Cessna."

Chapter Thirty

Lisbeth walked around the kitchen, preparing the table for breakfast. The euphoria of winning the Chambers Trophy was a faint memory. She and her father spent the entire week consoling her mother.

Hattie continued her rant that started when her daughter announced her move to Kansas and her job as a test pilot. "I don't know why you are doing this to me." She stirred the eggs in the iron skillet. "When I'm dead I want you to look at me in my casket and know you helped put me there."

She inhaled a deep breath and closed her eyes. "Ma, that's the worst thing you've ever said to me."

"Well, this is the worst thing you've done to me." She spooned eggs into a bowl. "And Paul—you didn't know he had a girlfriend while you flitted around with him all over the country? I raised you better than this."

She set the table with plates, cups and saucers, and silverware. "No, Ma, I didn't know. The engagement was a surprise to us all."

"How could you not know?" Her mother pulled her apron to her eyes and dried them.

She walked to Hattie, put her hands on her shoulders and turned her mother's face up so she could look in her eyes. "Ma, you've got to get a hold of yourself. Nothing you do or say is going to change anything. I'm moving to Wichita to start a new job, and

Paul is getting married."

"Why can't you stay here? You've got a job and a home. We'll let you stay here the rest of your life. Don't leave us." She sobbed into the apron.

Jacob entered the kitchen. "Hattie, enough. Leave the girl alone." He embraced his wife and rubbed his hand on her back. "It's all right. She'll come back to visit often."

She poured coffee in cups and observed her father calm her mother. She hoped someday she'd find someone who loved her as much as her pa loved her ma. She wet a rag with warm water and passed the soft cloth to her father.

He wiped his wife's face. "Everything is going to work out, dear, you'll see."

****

Lisbeth sat at her desk; the sound of the oscillating fan drowned out any wails or cries from her mother. She made a mental note of the things she'd taken care of and the things she still needed to do before the move. She'd given her father orders to give Ruth Ann two thousand dollars of her prize money. He would tell his oldest daughter it was money he'd set aside for his children's college fund and since she was the only one who went to college, she should have it. Ruth Ann was expecting another baby and they needed a larger house. Lisbeth didn't need it; the five hundred would get her to Kansas, and her salary would pay her bills.

Hattie burst into the room and threw a newspaper on her desk. "Read this." She pointed to a short article.

She read through the retraction of the engagement announcement and checked the date at the top. "Where'd you get this?"

Hattie sat on the bed. "Paul's downstairs talking to Jacob. He wants to see you."

Her breakfast churned in her stomach. "I don't want to see him."

Her mother grabbed her hand. "If you don't talk to him and get the full story, you'll regret it the rest of your life."

Her thumb slipped into her mouth and she chewed the nail. She jerked her hand away and clenched her fists. "I'll be down in a few minutes."

Hattie went to the door, turned, and walked back to her daughter. She put her arms around her and stroked her hair.

She hugged her mother, knowing this silent apology was the only one she would receive.

She combed her hair and stared in the mirror. She didn't bother to put on make-up or lipstick. *What does it matter, anyway?* She descended the stairs and stopped in the parlor door.

In two strides, he had her in his arms. "I'm sorry," he whispered. He turned to the Douglases. "I hope you don't mind—I'm taking your daughter for a short drive this morning, if she'll go with me." His eyes searched hers.

Standing so close to him stroked the ache in her core. She cursed herself for feeling it. "A short drive is fine." She grabbed her purse.

He situated her in the passenger seat and didn't say a word until he parked the car in the parking lot of New Hope Baptist Church. He silenced the ignition and pulled her toward him, placing a tender kiss on her lips. "I'm sorry, Lisbeth."

She searched his eyes for truth. "I knew you had

someone else." She willed her tears to stay put.

He touched her face. "I didn't have anyone else, not really." He put his hands on the steering wheel and clenched his fists. "I never lied to you, I omitted some important things, but I didn't lie."

She stared, waiting for him to speak.

He faced her, ready to tell the truth. "Kathleen and I were…um…lovers. She thought we would get married, our parents thought we would get married, hell, all our friends thought it. I guess I believed it too, although I was in no hurry. She dated other men, but I didn't care. I didn't know what love was until…until you."

She scooted to the middle of the seat and touched his arm.

He pulled away. "I'm not done." He stared out the front windshield. "All my life, I've wanted to please my father. He wanted me to marry Kathleen because her father is the richest oil man in Wichita. He wanted me to work for Beech to get flight time and experience, so I could work at Trans World Airlines."

She settled in her seat with her hands in her lap. "Sounds like your father had big plans for your life. A life most people would give their right arm for."

He pulled her close. "I don't want any of that, never did, although I didn't realize it until I moved here and met you. I want you, Lisbeth Rose, only you." He kissed her.

She opened her mouth and welcomed his deep kiss; her body betrayed her and begged for more. She wrung herself free of his embrace. "What else have you not told me?"

He cradled her hands in his. "Before my mother

died, she cut my father out of the will. The house, money, her entire estate, she left to me. My father contested it, unsuccessfully."

"Your father isn't the nicest man I've ever met, but you'd think his wife would leave him her estate." She remembered how he'd stared at her, and the things he said still gave her cold chills.

"Mom told me on her death bed he'd wasted the last of her money on gambling and other women. She got her revenge." He touched her cheek. "It doesn't matter about the money or the house; all that matters is you and me." He started the car. "I have one more stop to make before I take you home."

She stared out the car window and digested the information Paul told her. She recognized the familiar scenery as they headed toward Andrews Field. Aside from holding her hand and side glances, the ride was quiet.

He pulled in the drive and parked beside the Twin Beech. He opened her door and took her hand as she exited the car. He pulled a box from his pocket and got down on one knee.

She put her hand over her heart and stepped back. *This can't be happening.* His thumb and forefinger lifted the lid on the box. She stared at a huge diamond ring.

"I fell in love with you the first time I saw you here in this parking lot. Will you marry me and make me the happiest man on earth?"

She wanted to say yes, but he needed to know her plans. "Yes, yes. I'll marry you. But there's something I didn't tell you. I got the test pilot job at Cessna."

He swung her around. "I didn't tell you either, I got

an engineering job at Cessna. I'll design the planes and make sure they are safe for my test pilot wife to fly."

"Close your eyes." He guided her around the plane to the pilot side. "Open them."

Lisbeth Rose in cursive letters was written on the airplane. She touched the side of the plane. "Why's my name on it?"

"It's my wedding gift to you so you can fly home and see your family whenever you want. I know how much Saplingville means to you."

She touched her name tentatively in case the paint might rub off. "You were pretty confident I'd say yes."

He kissed her neck and whispered in her ear, "I wasn't leaving here without you."

A word about the author...

Before fulfilling her dream of being a published romance writer, Jane Lewis worked as a freelance musician and teacher, and an analyst and manager for a large railroad company. She is a native of Atlanta and lover of all things southern. She graduated from Kennesaw State University, Kennesaw, Georgia with a Bachelor of Arts degree in Music.

When she isn't writing her next romance, she enjoys cooking, tending her rose garden, playing music, yoga, and bowling with her real-life hero, her husband.

She and her husband live in a suburb outside of Atlanta. She is a PAN member of Romance Writers of America and Georgia Romance Writers. She was a 2016 finalist in the Hearts Through History, Post-Victorian/World War II category, for her first romance novel, *Love at Five Thousand Feet*.

www.janelewisauthor.com

Thank you for purchasing
this publication of The Wild Rose Press, Inc.

For questions or more information
contact us at
info@thewildrosepress.com.

The Wild Rose Press, Inc.
www.thewildrosepress.com